SECRETS FROM THE PAST

Corynne West, employed by wealthy businessman Grant Grantham, discovers that someone has a grudge against him and that there is some mystery about the death of his wife, two years previously. Corynne finds that she is falling in love with Grant, but realizes that his past has left him suspicious of women. She is determined to help him overcome his doubts, but will it help him if the secrets are revealed?

SHEILA ACKERMAN

SECRETS FROM THE PAST

Complete and Unabridged

LINFORD
Leicester

First published in Great Britain in 1993 by
Robert Hale Limited
London

First Linford Edition
published November 1994
by arrangement with
Robert Hale Limited
London

British Library CIP Data

Ackerman, Sheila
    Secrets from the past.—Large print ed.—
Linford romance library
I. Title II. Series
823.914 [F]

ISBN 0–7089–7612–3   100

Published by
F. A. Thorpe (Publishing) Ltd.
Anstey, Leicestershire

Set by Words & Graphics Ltd.
Anstey, Leicestershire
Printed and bound in Great Britain by
T. J. Press (Padstow) Ltd., Padstow, Cornwall

This book is printed on acid-free paper

1

CORYNNE WEST struggled out of the crowded train and dumped her heavy case on the platform, looking round expectantly. The few people waiting took no notice of her.

Suddenly a tousle-haired young man in jeans and T-shirt came hurrying through the entrance, and she watched him hopefully. He was tall, and broad-shouldered, with tightly curled brown hair, and a strong musclar body. His pleasant features were creased into an anxious frown. Seeing Corynne standing there he made straight for her, and skidded to a halt.

"Are you Miss West?" he panted. "Miss Corynne West? If you are I'm here to take you to Hazelcourt House."

"Yes, I am Corynne West," she agreed with a smile.

His rich brown eyes lit up with relief. "Let me have your case." He lifted it as though it weighed nothing. "Transport awaits."

Corynne looked at him with interest. He wasn't at all what she had expected. He was so friendly and casual, not at all like the shrewd businessman she had been expecting. This man seemed more of an open-air type, with his tanned skin and athletic movements.

He led the way out of the station, and towards a mini-bus bearing the words, 'Hazelcourt Conference Centre'. That was another surprise. She was supposed to be going to Hazelcourt House, not a conference centre.

"I don't understand. Is this your transport?"

"Sure is."

"Are you Mr Grantham?" she asked doubtfully, as he helped her into the bus, and settled her into the seat next to the driver's.

"Good Lord no," he laughed, as though it was a tremendous joke.

"Sorry, I should have introduced myself," he grinned boyishly. "My name is Alan Carey. I'm the manager of the conference centre."

"I still don't understand. Bill — Doctor Hallam told me that Mrs Grantham lived alone, but that her son came down for week-ends occasionally. He didn't tell me there was a conference centre here."

"You won't have anything to do with the running of the centre," Alan told her. "Mrs Grantham lives in Hazelcourt House, and the conference centre was built in the grounds. Grant has his head office in London. Since his wife died he prefers to live there."

"Yes, Bill — Doctor Hallam, told me that. He said Mr Grantham wanted someone who could act as his hostess occasionally, when he was entertaining guests at Hazelcourt House, but my primary duty will be to run the house, and look after his mother. She's a semi-invalid apparently."

"Yes, she is. Are you a nurse then?"

"I'm not a fully trained nurse, but I worked as an auxiliary for a while, while I was waiting for a place at secretarial college. That was how I met Bill."

"Corynne — you don't mind if I call you Corynne? Miss West is much too formal . . . "

He waited for her to reply.

"I'd rather you called me Rynne," she said. "Corynne's such a mouthful, and my friends always shorten it."

"So, that makes me a friend at least," he teased. "Rynne, it is. I was going to say — you'll always be welcome at the centre. I get time off, and sometimes we have an open evening, dancing, exhibitions, that kind of thing. In fact — there's an exhibition of modern art on this Saturday, tomorrow, to start next week's course, why don't you come? It would give you a chance to meet some of the local people, most of them will be there."

"Thanks," Corynne responded gratefully. "I shall have to see if Mrs

Grantham approves, and what she wants me to do, but it would be nice. Can I let you know later?"

"Sure. Contact me at the centre. I live there. I have a nice little flat in the main building."

"It's quite a long way from the town, isn't it?"

Corynne had been watching the countryside as they drove along. Once they left the town there seemed to be very few buildings of any sort, and little traffic.

"It's about twenty minutes drive. There's no bus service. We always meet people coming on a course, and take them back to the station afterwards, if they don't drive themselves."

"Were you expecting more people to be on my train then?"

"No." He looked surprised, then grinned. "Oh, you mean why did I bring the bus, not a car, don't you?"

"Well yes, it does seem rather big for just me. Did you think I'd have piles of luggage?"

5

He laughed. "It was Grant's idea. I suppose he thought it would reassure you, being met by a strange man. Made me look official."

"I see," Corynne said doubtfully.

"No you don't," Alan sighed. "I may as well tell you the truth. Grant didn't want it to look as though there was anything — personal, in your coming here. It's easier to start rumours than to stop them."

"I understand now. They're used to seeing you pick people up in the centre bus. Well, that was thoughtful of him," she said. "Do you come from round here yourself?"

"Yes. My mother still lives in the village."

"Have you lived here all your life then?"

"No," he chuckled wickedly. "I'm not quite a country bumpkin."

Corynne laughed too. "I wasn't hinting that you were," she said lightly. "I wondered what had made you stay when you said yourself there

6

isn't much work except for the centre. If it's always been your home I can understand it."

"I am rather fond of the place. I was glad of the chance to come back. When Grant first decided to open the centre he asked me if I'd like to run it for him. Mother always hoped I'd come back eventually, but she knew there wasn't much for me here, so naturally she was delighted. So was I, at the time."

He sounded as though he had changed his mind since, Corynne thought.

"That's the village of Hazelmere — that was," Alan said suddenly, as they drove through a group of houses and out again before she had time to really see anything.

"This is the centre entrance," he announced a few minutes later, pointing to a pair of gates. At the end of a long drive she could see an attractive whitewashed building that looked rather like a row of cottages. Beyond were larger buildings, all

7

blending in delightfully with the countryside.

"It looks very attractive," she enthused.

"Give Grant his due, he made sure that there was nothing that could give offence to anyone. The whole place was planned to blend in with existing buildings, and keep the country character. Even so there were some folk in the village who objected. He got his way though, he usually does."

He drove on along the narrow road for some considerable way, then turned in at a second pair of gates. "Here we are. Hazelcourt House."

She gazed at the house in awe. "It's so big," she breathed. "Bill didn't tell me it was so big."

"Don't let it scare you," he laughed. "Most of the rooms are shut up."

Alan stopped the bus in front of the heavy oak front door, and turned to her with a smile. "Well, you've arrived," he said, cheerfully. He helped her down from the bus, and carried her case to the door, ringing the bell. An elderly, motherly-looking woman opened the door, smiling warmly. Corynne liked her on sight.

"Martha, this is Corynne West," Alan announced. "Rynne, meet Martha Hawkes, housekeeper."

"Welcome to Hazelcourt House, my dear," Martha greeted her. "Come along in. I dare say you'd like to freshen up a bit before you meet Mr Grantham. My but it's hot, and you travelling such a long way."

"I do feel rather sticky," Corynne agreed, following her into a large, cool, marble-floored hall.

Martha turned to Alan. "Alan, carry Miss West's case upstairs for me, there's a love," she said with a twinkling smile.

Alan grinned. "For you, Martha — I'd do anything," he told her, and picked it up. "Which room?"

"The blue room. Third from the right top of the stairs," Martha told him. She turned back to smile at Corynne, as Alan bounded off up the impressive staircase.

"Miss West, you can go up to your room if you like, there's a wash-basin there, and the bathroom's further along the landing, or there's a cloakroom across the hall." Martha pointed to a door, almost hidden in a dark recess.

"The cloakroom will be fine," Corynne said. "I'll only be a moment." She walked towards it.

"Take your time, love," Martha said, and turned away, only to jerk round with a gasp of alarm as a hard voice echoed through the hall.

"Alan, how many times have I told you not to park that damned bus right outside the front door? And what do you think you're doing upstairs?"

Alan was just on his way back down, and he continued to walk slowly and deliberately, while the man who had called out strode towards the foot of the stairs and stood waiting for him.

Steely blue eyes glittered in a tautly angry, lean face. The man's mouth was a tight hard line, and he stood stiff and challenging until Alan reached him.

Corynne stood motionless, aware of the tension in the atmosphere. Neither man saw her, in the depths of the recess, they only had eyes for each other. Alan seemed wary, but unafraid, and stood smiling slightly in front of his challenger.

They were well matched, their height almost identical, but the newcomer was slightly the slimmer of the two, his shoulders not quite as broad as Alan's. Even so he looked as though he could be a formidable opponent. He stood aggressively poised, a stance that suggested finely-toned muscles, and athletic prowess.

Like challenging stags they faced each other, and Corynne wondered what could have caused such a confrontation. The actual accusation was so trivial that the situation seemed ludicrously over-dramatic.

"Back off, Grant," Alan said quietly. "I just brought your mother's new secretary from the station, and Martha asked me to carry her case up to her room. The bus has only been there for a few minutes, and it's not in anyone's way. That isn't why you're trying to pick a fight though, is it? Why don't you come out with what's really on your mind?"

"Alan, don't . . . " Martha whispered, then turned away as though she couldn't bear to watch the two men.

Corynne stood watching, expecting the two to come to blows at any moment, and she could hardly believe it when the newcomer, who she knew now must be Grant Grantham himself, suddenly broke into hard laughter.

"Sorry, Alan," he said, his voice slightly unsteady. "You're right, it's not you I'm angry with." He paused, and then added grimly, "At least I hope it isn't you. If it is then you're the one who should be coming out with whatever it is behind the campaign of hate."

"Apology accepted," Alan said with

a chill smile. "You picked the wrong man to take your temper out on, Grant. One day you're going to pick the wrong time too, and when that happens — watch out."

To Corynne's surprise Grant took a step backward, almost as though he was retreating, and his expression tightened. "I'll remember," he said quietly, then turned on his heel and strode away down the hall. He opened a door, then looked over his shoulder.

"Martha, I'll be in the library when Miss West is ready," he said brusquely, and strode into the room, slamming the door behind him.

"What was all that about?" Corynne asked. She moved towards Alan, who stiffened at the sight of her.

"I'm sorry you had to hear that," he said huskily. "He's been in a foul mood all morning. There was a story in the local papers about him, and he seems to think I had something to do with it. I didn't of course, but I don't think he's altogether convinced. Don't let it put you off. He's only that tough with me."

"Why?" The question was out before she could stop it.

Alan shrugged. "That's something that only Grant knows," he said brusquely. "Forget it, Rynne. It won't affect you I promise. He keeps it well under control usually, but there are times when I think that he deliberately tries to provoke me. It's as though he wants a show-down, but loses his nerve and backs off at the last moment, the way he just did. Only Grant doesn't scare easily. It doesn't add up."

"Would you back off if he didn't?"

Alan's eyes narrowed, and for a moment his boyishness gave way to a hard calculating awareness.

"You're a smart girl," he said lightly. "No, I don't think I would, and I'd rather not put it to the test. It might be better if you don't say anything about witnessing that little scene. He didn't know you were there, and neither did I. I thought you'd gone into the cloakroom."

"I won't say anything. I'd better tidy up. Mr Grantham will be wondering where I am."

Corynne hurried into the little cloakroom and splashed water on her face, cooling her fevered skin, then quickly repaired the ravages of the journey, and tidied her long dark hair. She went back into the hall and Martha came bustling towards her.

"Come on, love. I'll take you to Mr Grantham," she said, leading the way across the hall.

Martha tapped on the door through which Grant Grantham had disappeared, and waited for his brusque, "Come in," before opening it and giving Corynne an encouraging push into the room.

"Mr Grantham, Miss West is here," she announced.

"Thank you, Martha. Would you bring us some tea. I'm sure Miss West would like some after the journey," Grant Grantham said with a smile, looking up from the papers and books that were spread over a large desk in front of him.

"I certainly would. Thank you," Corynne said warmly. That smile had taken her by surprise and she felt her heart start pounding wildly, and a strange quiver running through her body making her limbs feel unsteady. In the gloom of the hall she had seen a much older, harder man, but she could see now, in the brightly sunlit room, that he couldn't be much more than in his late thirties.

His features were even, his face lean, but there was no harshness or anger left. His eyes were a vivid blue, and against his tanned skin they had a compelling intensity. The smile had softened his mouth, making his lips look fuller, with a well-defined shape, and his hair was lighter than she had thought, not quite blonde, but a light brown, with golden glints, and thickly waved. One lock had tumbled over his forehead, and he put up a slender, but strong looking hand, and deftly flicked it back into place. Suddenly the smile vanished.

She wished he would smile again, he'd looked so much more approachable, but now his mouth was tight and thin again, and the blue eyes had lost the sparkle that had made them so compelling. Her racing heart steadied to an even beat, and she saw him again as a cold, calculating man. She felt cheated.

"Do sit down. Did you have a comfortable journey?" he asked, waiting while Martha bustled in with a tray, and clearing a space for her to set it down on the desk with a quick sweep of his hand.

"The first part was comfortable, until I had to change to the local train at Portsmouth," she answered, trying to make sense of what she had seen. He had seemed so friendly and relaxed for that first moment or two, then suddenly changed.

He nodded. He seemed preoccupied,

she thought, only part of his attention on what she was saying. He poured the tea, and looked at her. "Milk? Sugar?"

"Just a dash of milk please. No sugar."

"Alan met you all right, I hope."

"Yes, thank you. Alan took good care of me."

One eyebrow lifted slightly, as though he was questioning her remark, then he stood up, walking round the desk to hand her the cup. She was very aware of the power of his personality as their hands touched momentarily, and she was annoyed with herself for feeling strangely disturbed by his nearness. She was glad when he returned to his seat.

"I'm sorry I couldn't interview you personally before you came here but since we both know Doctor Hallam very well I was quite happy to accept his recommendation, and I assume that he told you everything that you needed to know, otherwise you wouldn't be here."

"Yes, Doctor Hallam explained that you want someone to look after your mother, and help in running the house, when you're away," she said. "I've had no actual experience in such a position, but I'm sure that I can cope efficiently."

"I was expecting an older woman," he said bluntly. "Bill Hallam gave me the impression that you were extremely efficient, and able to cope with any situation that might arise."

So that was why the smile had vanished so abruptly, Corynne thought resentfully.

"I'm twenty-six, and my age, qualifications, and details of work experience, are clearly stated in my C.V.," she said sharply. "If you didn't take the trouble to read it properly that is not my fault."

His eyebrows rose, and he seemed about to say something caustic, then suddenly he smiled again, and she relaxed thankfully.

"Sorry. I did read the C.V. I assure

you, but somehow I had imagined you as a much more mature person, from the details given. Rather formidable, in fact," he said, with a soft laugh. "I apologize if I seemed rude, Miss West. I took a chance in inviting you to come without meeting you first, but you have excellent qualifications, and a personal recommendation from a mutual friend."

"I took a chance too, in coming here when I knew very little about you," she countered. "I took Doctor Hallam's word for it that I would find the position suitable, even though it was something that I hadn't had experience of. I understood that Mrs Grantham owns the house, and that you are an infrequent visitor."

It came out as almost an accusation, something that she had not intended, and she could see that he had reacted to the implication. She watched his expression harden again, and a chill glitter dull the blue of his eyes, but his self-control was evident too.

"You are quite right," he said evenly. "However, it is still my home, and I have been very concerned about mother being here alone so much. Alan Carey keeps an eye on her, but he has a full-time job running the conference centre. I need someone who will be in the house all the time, and can cope with any emergency that might arise."

"I'm sure that I shall be well able to cope," Corynne told him stiffly.

He hesitated, and glanced away, then looked at her very intently. "Doctor Hallam assured me that I can depend on your discretion in keeping to yourself anything that you might hear. I'm sure that you understand."

Unexpectedly she felt sorry for him. "I do understand," she assured him. "Your secrets are safe with me."

He looked startled, then angry. "It's nothing like that," he said curtly. "It's — just that mother has become very fanciful, and tends to unburden herself to anyone who'll listen to her. Unfortunately many of the things she worries about are all in her imagination."

"You mean she's — demented?" Corynne could not help letting her shock show, and Grant frowned at her.

"No, Bill assures me that she's quite sane, she just — exaggerates. Everything she reads about me in the local papers she interprets as a threat. She insists that someone is trying to kill me. It's ridiculous of course. I've made enemies. It's inevitable in business, but no one would go to that length to get rid of me."

"I should hope not," Corynne said.

He smiled, sadly. "There isn't much we can do about it, except make sure that she doesn't talk to the wrong people. That's why it's so important that I find someone who I can trust absolutely. Mother becomes very distressed at times. She's had the police here more than once."

"Mr Grantham, I will be discreet, and I do understand. It must be very worrying for you."

His explanation had sounded so plausible, she thought, but was it? Was there really some dark secret from the past that overshadowed his life even now? Strangely enough she felt more compassion than doubt. Whatever the secret, he was suffering, and would probably go on suffering, unless . . .

"You have a month to decide," he said crisply, getting to his feet. "Martha will show you your room, and explain the household. Mother is resting, you'll meet her after dinner. She takes her meals in her own room. She prefers to eat alone these days. We can go into details later if there's anything you want to know."

She stood up and put the empty cup on the tray, her hand a little unsteady. "You'll be staying for a while then?" she said, making it sound as though she wasn't really interested.

"I shall be staying until Sunday afternoon, then I have to go back to London. You can always contact me by phone if there's anything you can't handle. By the way, Doctor Hallam is dining with us this evening. I expect you'll be pleased to see him."

"Yes, I shall," Corynne smiled. "Thank you, Mr Grantham. I hope that I can give satisfaction."

For a moment their eyes met, and unexpectedly he returned her smile. She felt a shock run through her, as though she had touched a live wire, and turned away hastily, hoping that he hadn't noticed her strange reaction.

"I hope you do," he said quietly, making her wonder just what the soft words had meant, and if she had read more into his response than he'd intended. When she turned to look at him his features were inscrutable, and, without another word, he strode forward and opened the door for her to leave.

She hurried out in search of Martha, feeling strangely disturbed.

2

CORYNNE found Martha in the kitchen, busily rolling pastry.

"Sit down for a moment while I get this in the oven, Miss West," she said cheerfully. "Pour yourself a cup of tea. I daresay you could drink another one. There's china on the dresser." She waved a floury hand at the huge pine dresser behind her.

"Thanks, I'd love another one," Corynne accepted gratefully. She sat at the other end of the huge, well-scrubbed table, watching Martha. "Do please call me Rynne, it's short for Corynne. Miss West sounds much too formal."

"Rynne it is then, and Martha suits me fine," Martha smiled. "What do you think of Hazelcourt House then?" she asked.

"It's lovely, but a lot bigger than I expected."

"Only the ground and first floors in the main building are used. The top floor, what used to be the servants' quarters, had been shut up for years, and so have the east and west wings," Martha told her. "It's hard enough keeping the place up together as it is."

"How do you manage? You can't do all the housework youself, surely?"

"Lord love you, no." Martha laughed. "We have a couple of women in from the village for cleaning. I suppose you'll be taking charge of things like hiring staff and paying the bills and suchlike now."

"Well, yes, I shall be responsible for the everyday running. Who did it before, did you?"

"Not me. I'm only the housekeeper and cook. I never had nothing to do with the bills and such. Mrs Grantham, she saw to all that side of things, before she was took ill. Then the master saw to it, but he's away so much. When Mrs Grantham got well enough not to need a proper nurse he decided to get someone to surpervise things, and keep her company. Doctor Hallam said he knew of someone, and — here you are."

"I think I'm going to like it here. It seems very quiet and peaceful," Corynne said.

Martha sniffed. "Aye, until Master Grant and young Alan get on at each other. You saw them just now."

"Why does Alan work for him if they don't get on?" Corynne ventured.

Martha sniffed again. "You might well ask. I don't know, I'm sure. It's odd, young Alan's such a good-natured lad, always ready to help folk. He's always been well liked. Him and Master Grant used to be like brothers when they were boys. They're the same age, Alan and Master Grant, give or take a couple of months. Thirty-six this year, the pair of them."

"I thought Mr Grantham was older than that," Corynne remarked, surprised. "And Alan seems much younger."

"Aye, well, Master Grant never got over losing that pretty wife of his."

"What happened? Was she taken ill?"

"No Miss," Martha sighed, and shook her head sadly. "Tragedy it was. She went swimming one summer evening, and drowned."

"That's dreadful."

Martha nodded. "He took it real hard at the time. They were living here in the house then, with the children. The boy, Raoul, he's two now, and the little girl, Lucy, she's three, four next month. Beautiful children they are, Miss. They live with their other grandparents in France now."

"He must miss them all very much. How long ago did it happen?"

"Nearly two years. It wasn't long after Raoul was born it happened. He's got over it more or less, but it left him bitter. Don't be too ready to criticize if he seems a bit — hard, Rynne. He's got good reason believe me."

"I won't judge him too harshly,"

Corynne promised. "Why do you call him Master Grant? It sounds so old-fashioned."

Martha nodded, and smiled agreeably. "Prap's it does. I watched him grow from a baby, always called him Master Grant when he was a lad, and I suppose I just can't stop. I been at the house since I was a girl fresh from school. Started as housemaid, and worked up to cook."

"Do you mind me coming here?" Corynne asked guiltily. "You seem to have managed very well on your own, until now."

"Bless you, love. I don't want the responsibility. I told Master Grant that I'd be happy to stop on as cook, long as I don't get no interference."

She looked at Corynne expectantly.

"That's a relief, since I can't cook," Corynne told her. "Don't worry, I'll stay well clear of the kitchen."

"I didn't mean it like that, love. Course you can come in the kitchen, any time you like. I just meant — well, that nurse, she was always fussing round, telling me how to do things. Mrs Grantham must have this, or Mrs Grantham mustn't have that, as if I didn't know what the old lady likes. I been cooking for her long enough."

"I expect she had to be put on a diet while she was ill," Corynne tried to soothe Martha. "I'd better go and unpack. What time is dinner?"

"7.30. but when Master Grant's home he usually has a drink in the sitting-room first. Come down about seven."

"I don't know if I should. I'm not a guest."

"Master Grant made it quite clear that you're to be treated like one of the family, same as young Alan. He invited Doctor Hallam to dinner tonight special to make you feel at home, said you'd be glad of a familiar face in a strange place."

"That was very thoughtful of him," Corynne said wonderingly. She was surprised that he had been so considerate, and wondered what other surprises might be in store for her. There was more to Grant Grantham than the ill-tempered grouch she had at first suspected him to be.

"Does Mr Grantham dress for dinner?"

"No," Martha shook her head. "He just wears an ordinary suit, unless it's a special occasion. Sometimes he brings business people down for the weekend, then it's all posh and formal. Just put on a decent frock, love. There's nothing to dress up for these days. The old lady never entertains, an' when Master Grant's not here you'll be all on your own meal-times. You can eat in the kitchen with me then, if you like."

"That sounds like a good idea. No point in you having to set a table just for me," Corynne agreed readily. "Mr Grantham told me that his mother always has her meals in her room."

"Aye, the poor lady. She's a bit sensitive about being partially paralysed, makes it hard for her to manage, but she's that stubborn, likes to do things herself, not have folks trying to help her. Don't ever let her think you're sorry for her love, pretend you haven't noticed if she's struggling with something. She won't thank you for what she calls interfering."

"I'll try to remember. Is there plenty of hot water? I'd like a bath."

"All the hot water you want. Master Grant had the place modernized, put in gas central heating instead of the old boilers. Wanted to make sure his mother would be comfortable." Martha looked at the big clock on the wall. "Time I was seeing about dinner. Nice joint of beef, new potatoes, and veg from the garden. There's apple tart and cream to follow."

"Sounds great," Corynne said.

Martha eyed her critically. "Look as though you could do with feeding up. Put some flesh on those bones. You young people don't know how to eat properly these days, all that convenience food."

"I'm quite fat enough, thank you," Corynne laughed. "I'll go and sort myself out then. Which room is mine? You needn't bother to come up, I can find it."

"Thanks, love. It's the third on the right from the top of the stairs. It's all furnished in blue, you can't mistake it. I'll pop up later and see if there's anything you want."

"I'm sure it'll suit me very well," Corynne assured her. "See you later."

She walked out through the hall, and up the stairs, humming a merry tune. Martha was so friendly that she already felt that she belonged here. She counted the doors along the corridor and opened the third along.

The room was bright and airy, with tall windows overlooking the garden. The carpet was a soft slate blue, scattered with deeper blue fluffy rugs, the walls papered with a delicate design of blue flowers on a white background, matching the chintz curtains and bedspread. Blue was definitely not for a boy here, it was an utterly feminine room, and she loved it immediately.

It was still only five o'clock, and she unpacked, hanging her few clothes in the enormous wardrobe, where they looked lost. She would have to get the rest of her things sent on, if she took the job permanently.

There was a wash-basin in the room, and thick fluffy blue towels on the rail ready for her. Even the soap was blue, she noticed. She slipped out of her clothes, staring at herself critically in the full-length wall mirror. Brown eyes stared back at her solemnly.

How could Martha have thought her thin? she wondered. She was reasonably well proportioned for her height of five feet six. She made a silent vow to avoid too much of Martha's rich food.

Turning away from the mirror with a sigh, she donned her cotton house-coat, then picked up her toilet bag and the bath towel and went in search of the bathroom, wishing that she'd thought to ask Martha which door it was.

As she stood on the wide landing, looking rather helplessly at the row of closed doors, one of them opened, and Grant Grantham came striding out wearing nothing but a towel wrapped round his waist.

He stopped and stood staring at her with an expression of sheer disbelief, then suddenly started laughing, hastily clutching the towel more securely.

"Damn it, I forgot you were here," he said shakily. "I shall remember to be more discreet in future."

She eyed him thoughtfully, feeling a strange yearning to touch his tanned, moist skin, and feel the muscles that rippled in his shoulders. There wasn't an ounce of superfluous fat on him, and his movements were fluid and sensuous.

She realized that he was studying her in return, and she knew that the thin cotton of her house-coat was clinging to her hot body in a revealing way. She put her hand to the wrapover, drawing it tighter round her breasts, knowing immediately that it was a mistake. The fabric tightened over her nipples, and they rose, thrusting against the covering.

She fought against the flooding warmth that spread through her body, knowing that nature was telling her all too clearly that she was sexually aroused by this man. They stared at each other silently, in that strange telepathy of nature and summer heat.

Grant was the first to succumb to the irresistible urge, and with a soft groan, that was almost a cry of despair, he stepped forward, and jerked her roughly into his arms. His lips were cool at first, but the message they gave burned into her mind and through her trembling body like a flood of consuming fire, leaving her helpless.

His hands tore the flimsy robe down from her shoulders, only the sash preventing him from baring her body completely. He paused to kiss her neck, pulling her against his chest, crushing her breasts against his body, and running his hands over her shoulders and back in savage exploration. She could feel the want in him, and her own matched his.

She had no thought for right or wrong, no thought for what they were doing. All that mattered was the agonizing desire for him.

They did not hear Martha's light footsteps crossing the hall and coming up the stairs. They heard nothing until her sudden wild scream made them jerk apart in guilty shock.

"Oh, Master Grant. I'm sorry. I'm so sorry," Martha gasped. She was standing at the top of the stairs, staring at them, wide-eyed.

There was no way of pretending innocence. His towel was on the floor at his feet, and Corynne was naked to the waist, her robe held only by the sash, like the revealing draperies of a Greek statue. Martha stumbled away, back down the stairs.

"Oh my God," Grant groaned,

snatching up the towel and covering himself, while Corynne struggled to draw the clinging fabric up over her fevered body.

"My God, I don't know what came over me." He took a deep shuddering breath, running his hands over his damp hair, and turning his back on Corynne. "I must have been crazy, but — you let me, damn you." He jerked round, his eyes blazing. "You let me," he accused bitterly.

"Yes, I let you," she said, her voice a strained whisper. She backed away, pressing herself against the wall, staring at him as though he was some hideous creature from a nightmare. "I don't believe it, but — it happened. It really did happen. You took me by surprise."

"I took myself by surprise too," he said wryly, and his dry humour in that tense moment helped to break the spell of guilt.

She shook her head doubtfully. "I can't stay here now, not after — Martha saw us like that. She was so upset . . . "

"Because she thought she was intruding, probably."

"If she hadn't?" Corynne clutched her robe tighter.

"If she hadn't . . . " he echoed, taking a step closer.

"No, get away from me. Leave me alone," she cried wildly, forcing her trembling limbs to move. She stumbled towards the door of her room, and clawed it open.

"Corynne, wait," he said sharply. "We've got to talk . . . "

"There's nothing to talk about. I'll leave first thing in the morning, and until then I would rather stay in my room."

"Don't be silly. There's no need for that," he said roughly. "I know we can't pretend it didn't happen, but there's no need for us to panic. Don't worry about Martha, she's been here too long to gossip, and we're both consenting adults, after all." He frowned, his features hardening. "I hope you agree that we did both consent?"

"Yes, of course," Corynne agreed huskily.

"Good. Let's try to behave like sensible people."

She turned and looked at him wonderingly. He seemed quite calm now, and was keeping his distance.

"What can you possibly say that would make any difference? I feel — cheap, and — degraded."

"Because I found you attractive enough to want to make love to you?" he laughed caustically.

Because I wanted you to, she thought to herself miserably, staring at him in silence. She didn't understand what had happened. They were practically strangers, but she'd wanted it more than she'd ever wanted anything before, and she hadn't cared about the consequences. The knowledge was frightening.

Her silence seemed to anger him. "Damn it, it was only a kiss," he shouted savagely. "You can't tell me that it's the first time a man has ever kissed you, or touched you. You didn't shy away like an affronted virgin . . . "

"Stop it. Stop it," she screamed at him wildly. "Just leave me alone. I can't stay here. I can't . . . "

She jerked open the bedroom door, but before she could get inside his hand closed over her wrist, jerking her round to face him.

"Please don't be too angry with me," he said curtly. "It will never happen again, I give you my word. I'm not going to make excuses, I can't, it was a moment of madness, but mother needs you, and you'll hardly ever see me, I promise. I don't spend much time here, there's nothing here for me since . . . "

He broke off, and turned his head away, as though he did not want her to see his face.

"Martha told me about your wife," she said, trying to help him. She was very aware of his hand on her wrist, and knew that she dared not stay near him any longer. She jerked free, and darted into her room, partly closing the door.

41

"Give me time to think," she said, peering at him through the gap. "I don't know what to do."

"All right. Can we just pretend that nothing happened, for this evening? Bill Hallam will wonder what's going on if you stay in your room. I could put him off of course, it's up to you."

"There's no need. I'll come down for dinner. I don't want to make things any more difficult than they are. I just need time to think . . . "

She closed the door on him, and leaned against it trembling. She heard him pad along the landing, then a door slammed, and only then did she dare make a dash for the bathroom, scooping up the toilet bag that she had dropped on the way, and locking the door carefully. Not that she was afraid of Grant Grantham, she was more afraid of her own reactions.

She ran the bath, sprinkling in exotically perfumed bath crystals from a large jar on the shelf beside it, and stretched out in the fragrant water

42

trying to relax and trying to make sense of the alarming way she had felt, pressed against Grant Grantham's lean body. It still seemed like the most wonderful sensation she had ever experienced.

From the moment she had first seen him, striding so grimly along the hall, angry and determined, she had felt a strange fascination about him. It wasn't his looks, though he was good-looking enough, it was something about the man himself, the brooding eyes, and guarded expression, that had made her want to fathom the depths of his mind. To understand the complexity that was Grant Grantham.

With a sudden blaze of anguish she realized that already she was dangerously attracted to him, and she didn't know whether to be glad or sorry that Martha had interrupted them.

She went back to her room and flicked through her meagre wardrobe, finally settling on a plain sleeveless dress of a soft jade green that brought out the colour of her brown eyes, and the creamy gold of her skin. It was a simple style, with a tight-fitting bodice flaring out into a full swirling calf-length skirt, accentuating the slimness of her waist.

By the time she went downstairs she had achieved an outward serenity at least. She would cling to the thought that after all it had only been a kiss, and only she knew what she had felt. Grant seemed ready to blame himself, in spite of that agonized accusation.

She remembered his bitter voice. "You let me," he had challenged, and she could only agree. He had seemed almost afraid. Now, in retrospect, she was more aware of the nuances of tone in that cry. The sense of shock, as though he had been trying to convince himself that it had not been entirely his fault. Did he have some reason to fear being blamed?

Stop it, she told herself, frightened by the way her thoughts were turning.

Of course he was upset. If she'd resisted he'd never have touched her. She could have stopped him the moment she'd realized what was happening, but she didn't. It wasn't his fault. He hadn't tried to rape her . . .

"Corynne, are you all right?"

She jerked into movement, realizing that she was standing in a daze, halfway down the broad staircase. Grant was just crossing the hall towards the main doorway, but stopped when he saw her standing there.

She hurried on down the stairs. "I'm fine," she told him, meeting his questioning gaze steadily.

He was wearing dark trousers, white shirt with a bow tie, and a light linen jacket, and in spite of the heat he looked immaculate.

"I've just had a word with Martha," he said evenly. "I was right, she was upset because she thought she was in the wrong."

"How did you explain . . . ?"

"I didn't offer any explanation. I

thought it best to let her draw her own conclusions about what she saw. It is our business after all, and she's very much the faithful family retainer. Her loyalty is almost unbelievable. The Grantham's can do no wrong in her eyes."

"She's too good to be true."

He smiled sadly. "In a way, yes, but she's no fool. She makes up her own mind about what she hears and sees, and her loyalty isn't blind. Martha is a law unto herself, and she soon lets you know if you step outside her boundaries. She likes you, Corynne. I hope you don't mind if I call you Corynne. Miss West hardly seems appropriate now."

"Hardly," she agreed with a nervous smile. "My friends call me Rynne."

"Rynne," he smiled. "I hope you'll call me Grant. Come into the sitting-room and have a drink. I don't know about you, but I could do with one."

3

UNEXPECTEDLY Corynne felt at ease. Grant's matter of fact way of dealing with a difficult moment had overcome any embarrassment, and she began to think that after all that moment of weakness had been no bad thing. They now shared something very special, and there was no going back. It might have taken her very much longer to have broken through his reserve normally.

He led the way into a comfortable room, with magnificent bay windows, and a patio door open to the terrace beyond, and a view of the gardens.

"This is a lovely house," she said, settling herself into one of the big settees, while Grant went to the cocktail cabinet.

"What would you like?"

"White wine please, preferably

medium sweet, if you have it."

He brought the wine to her in a delicate cut glass goblet, and sat beside her, with a small whisky in his hand.

"Bill should be arriving at any minute. He's bringing a friend, Julie Lister. I think you'll like Julie, she's one of the receptionists at the health centre in Hazelbury. She's a local girl. Lives in the village with her parents."

"Bill told me the practice was trying to open a small surgery and clinic in the village itself," Corynne said.

"Yes, I think it's a splendid idea. They've always had to depend on the town practice, and it would make life a lot easier for the mothers with young children."

"You know, I hadn't realized that there were still places like Hazelmere left. No buses, no doctor, how do people manage?"

"They depend on each other a great deal. Someone will always rally round to help in an emergency, and the villagers are a very close-knit

48

community. Of course my family provided most of the employment years ago, plus a couple of small farms nearby. The Grantham estate was quite large originally, but every generation had to face death duties, and various other expenses. Upkeep of the house itself cost a fortune, and over the years most of the land was sold off. The centre grounds, and the garden of the house is all that remains."

"It seems such a pity."

"That's progress," he laughed rather caustically. "I was lucky. My father went into the hotel business, and was very successful. I've been able to expand even more with projects like the conference centre here, which brought some employment back for the local village."

"The villagers must be very grateful to you."

He shrugged. "You'd think so, wouldn't you. In fact I had the devil's own job to get local support for the project at first. Some of them were very much against it, said it would destroy the character of the village. I pointed out that there wouldn't be a village left soon, if people went on leaving as they had been. A lot of the young people were moving into Hazelbury."

They were making small-talk, and she was glad when the doorbell rang, and Grant went to answer it.

Corynne stood up as a bear of a man came shambling in. Bill Hallam looked more like an all-in wrestler than a doctor. Massively built, with a thatch of straw-coloured curls, and a bushy beard to match, he was grinning broadly. He was wearing baggy grey trousers, and a faded red shirt, open at the neck, with the sleeves rolled up.

"Forgive me for not dressing for the occasion," he bellowed. "It's far too hot to stand on ceremony, Grant. Hallo, Rynne, me old darling, how are you?"

Before she could dodge she was enveloped in his massive arms, and almost crushed. He planted a kiss on her cheek, then let her go so abruptly that she had to sit down again with a thump.

"Julie, come and meet an old friend of mine, Corynne West," he bellowed again, looking round vaguely. "Darn it girl, where have you got to?" He reached behind him and hauled forward the girl who had followed him in.

She was a complete contrast to Bill Hallam. Small, slender, and dark haired, she looked like a doll against his massive frame, and she was laughing as he pulled her into view. She was clearly well used to Bill Hallam's eccentricities.

"Julie, Rynne. Rynne, Julie," he introduced them airily. "You two are going to be great friends."

It sounded like an order.

"Bill, you don't change do you?" Corynne laughed at him happily. "It's good to see you again."

"Watch your step girl, you've got a reputation to live up to," he cautioned her. "I sang your praises to old Grant here, and he, poor fool, believed every word I told him. Thinks you're some kind of superwoman, don't you old man?"

He turned to Grant with a grin.

"No, I don't," Grant answered rather tetchily.

Bill's grin vanished, and he looked at Corynne doubtfully, then back at Grant.

Grant smiled tightly. "I accepted Corynne on her own merits," he told Bill. "I read her C.V. very carefully, and I think she's going to prove to be just what mother needs. I hope she doesn't find it too quiet, that's all. After the bright lights of Bristol it's going to seem pretty dull down here."

"Don't worry, she *wanted* a bit of peace and quiet, that's why I suggested her for the job, but I'll see that she meets people, and gets around," Bill grinned. "There's the centre too, plenty going on there."

Grant frowned, seemed about to reply, then turned and strode across the room. "What would you like to drink, Julie? The usual?" he called over his shoulder.

"Please," she answered. "Not much gin, Grant, and lots of tonic please."

She sat down beside Corynne on the settee. "Have you seen the village yet?" she asked.

"Only a brief glimpse as we came through from Hazelbury. It looks very pretty, and unspoilt. Grant told me you still live there."

"Yes, I'm not very far away from you," Julie agreed eagerly. "There aren't many single young people left now, and it'll be nice to know someone close. You'll be able to drive down when you're free."

"I haven't got a car."

"Oh but — you must have transport, you can't stay stuck out here all the time," Julie objected, and called over to Grant. "Grant, Corynne says she hasn't got a car. You can't let her stay

53

here without one."

Grant walked towards them, handing Julie her drink.

"You've got a driving licence haven't you, Corynne?" he asked.

"Yes, I have, and a car back home in Bristol, but I didn't fancy the long drive down in it. It's not exactly reliable."

"No problem. There are cars in the garage, you can take your pick. You'll need transport for shopping, and running errands for mother, and she might like a drive sometimes. She used to drive herself of course, but she can't any more."

"Thanks. That'll be great."

"Don't thank me, it goes with the job," he smiled, and turned away. "What'll it be then Bill? Orange juice or club soda?"

"There, that's settled then." Julie smiled happily. "It'll be fun having you around, Rynne."

"How long have you known Bill?" Corynne asked.

"About a year," Julie answered

readily. "But we've only been 'walking out' as my mother likes to call it, for about six months. He's like a cuddly bear isn't he." She smiled fondly. "He's a darned good doctor though, I have found that out. Have you known him long?"

Corynne sensed the unspoken question behind the one spoken aloud, and smiled understandingly.

"Years and years. He's been like a big brother to me, always there when I needed someone." She patted the other girl's hand. "Don't worry, I'm no competition. Bill isn't my type, and I'm not his. I know people joke about such things, but we really are just good friends."

Julie flushed a little. "Oh dear, is it that obvious?"

"Not really," Corynne assured her. "I just wanted to be sure that you knew the truth. I don't want to start off on the wrong foot, and I do want to be friends with you."

"Good," Julie said with obvious

satisfaction. "Bill said we'd get on well."

She glanced across to where the two men were standing, talking, by the open patio doors, then laughed loudly as Bill raised both hands, and held them out in front of him about two feet apart.

"Don't let him kid you Grant," she called. "It was a tiddler."

Bill looked round and grinned good-naturedly. "There's more to fishing than just catching fish," he retorted. "It's the peace of the river-bank, the open air, communing with nature."

"Telling tall stories," Julie supplemented, looking at Corynne with a mischievous smile. "Bill's just taken up fishing, but the fish don't seem to want to co-operate."

Bill grinned again. "Talking of tall stories, old boy," he said to Grant, "I see you've had another set-to with the press. Haven't you learned your lesson yet?"

"Whoops," Julie muttered, as Grant's

face stiffened, and he glared at Bill dangerously.

"Tact was never Bill's strong point," Corynne whispered, and waited anxiously as the two men stood staring at each other. "Talk about the proverbial bull in a china shop, Bill's your original elephant in a glass factory."

"I'd rather not discuss it Bill," Grant said in a warningly chill tone. "As usual they blew up what was a minor argument, into a full-scale fight. I asked the photographers to leave us alone, but you know what it's like, they have to get their pictures."

"They got a picture all right," Bill chuckled. "Is he suing?"

"I didn't touch the man, damn it." Grant's voice was getting louder, and his eyes glittered like blue steel.

Julie stood up and moved towards the two men, looking frightened, and Corynne watched, startled by the sudden change in Grant, and wondering just what he had done.

"That picture was a complete

fake," Grant declared furiously, then shrugged. His expression indicated angry resignation. "Damn it, the man shoved his camera right in my face, and I pushed him away. It was pure instinctive reaction. That photo was a trick shot, I know it looked as though my fist was about to connect with his face, but I was nowhere near."

"Calm down," Bill said gruffly.

Grant grimaced. "I know I shouldn't rise to the bait, but damn it, if you'd been hounded the way I was after Marianne's accident, wouldn't you be angry?"

Bill put a soothing hand on his shoulder, and turned him away from the room, urging him out onto the terrace.

Julie returned to her seat, and Corynne looked at her expectantly. "What was all that about?"

"Obviously you didn't see the morning papers."

"No. I bought a magazine to read on the train. The print gets all over you from the papers. Was there something about Grant in them then?"

"Yes, he was at some business dinner, with a rather beautiful girl. Poor Grant. I feel sorry for him really, he had a dreadful time when Marianne died. The papers hounded him, looking for a scandal. There were rumours that there'd been some kind of mystery about her death. Another man involved, you know the kind of thing. Most of it was in the local paper here luckily, or you'd have remembered."

"I didn't know anything about Grant, or Hazelcourt House, in those days," Corynne said. "If I did read anything I'd forgotten it."

"Didn't Bill tell you? — no, obviously he didn't." Julie frowned. "He should have warned you."

"Warned me about what?" Corynne asked faintly.

"Oh it's nothing really, just gossip, but you know how cruel people can be. Grant put a lot of people's backs up over the centre business, and there are some who'd love to see him brought down. It's spiteful, and petty, but that's the way it is in a small place. That's why he keeps away. His mother flatly refuses to leave Hazelmere, so he has to make the best of it."

"What exactly was in the papers this morning?"

Julie sighed. "It started out as the usual gossip column stuff, but he'd lost his temper when they wouldn't stop asking questions. There was a photo of Grant, apparently punching a photographer. You heard what he said, it was a fake, and I believe him. He's always being hounded by the press."

"It's so unfair," Corynne protested. "Why do they . . . " She broke off, as Martha came in to announce that dinner was ready. She tried to smile at the woman, but Martha refused to look at her directly. A little of her previous doubt returned, and she knew that the incident was far from over. There was going to be some difficult moments yet to come, if she did stay.

The meal was simple, and they served themselves. It was very much the kind of family meal that Corynne was used to at home, and she relaxed, and joined in the conversation. Grant seemed to be making an effort to be light-hearted, but at times she saw him sitting silent and preoccupied, until Bill jollied him into forced laughter over some outrageous remark. She was glad Bill was there.

With Bill around no one could be gloomy for long. He sat there in his shirt-sleeves, not caring what anyone thought of him, unselfconscious, and bubbling with the sheer joy of being alive. His exuberance was irresistible, yet, as Corynne knew very well, when help was needed he was the most considerate, and dependable of men.

When the meal was finished, Grant stood up. "Bill, take the girls through into the drawing-room, will you? I'll see if mother is ready to join us," he said, and strode out.

Bill escorted them back to the room

they had been in previously. Corynne sat waiting for Grant to return, feeling a little nervous, wondering what Mrs Grantham would be like, and when the door opened, and Grant appeared, pushing his mother in a wheel-chair, she stood up expectantly.

For a start Mrs Grantham was not the frail, white-haired old lady that Corynne had pictured. She appeared to be in the best of health. Her hair was a warm mid-brown, and braided elegantly on top of her head, like a coronet. Her eyes were the same deep blue as Grant's, and just as penetrating. She was wearing a long flowing gown of deep blue silk, with long sleeves, and looked very regal. Corynne had a moment of doubt, then she met those vivid blue eyes, and Mrs Grantham smiled.

The illusion of perfect health disappeared. One side of her face remained stiff and expressionless, and when she raised her hand towards Corynne, in a rather imperious gesture of greeting, the other slid awkwardly to her side.

"My dear, you must be Corynne West," Mrs Grantham said warmly, her speech a little distorted, but still clearly understandable. Corynne wondered what effort of will power had been behind that slow deliberate enunciation. From her brief spell in hospital she knew a little of the problems of stroke victims.

She moved closer, and grasped the outstretched hand, feeling the slender fingers close round her own with surprising strength.

"Bill has told me so much about you," Mrs Grantham went on, then paused for a moment, breathing heavily, a moment that revealed how weak she still was.

Her breathing eased, and she went on resolutely. "I'm sure we're going to get on very well, and I hope you'll be very happy at Hazelcourt. We'll leave the details until later, the week-end is a social occasion. I shall not expect you to do anything more than settle in and enjoy yourself."

"Thank you, I'm sure I shall be happy here, it's a lovely house," Corynne responded, taking an instant liking to her new employer.

The evening passed pleasantly. Mrs Grantham clearly enjoyed company and conversation, though several times when she mentioned past events, Grant quickly steered the conversation to a different subject.

It was only 10.30 when Mrs Grantham said regretfully, "I see it's my bedtime, and since my doctor is right beside me I can hardly disobey his orders. Corynne, I would like to have a little chat with you sometime in the morning, I think we should get to know each other. Will you come to my room?"

"Yes, of course." Corynne agreed readily. "What time would you like me to come?"

"Martha brings my breakfast at nine, and I like to take my time dressing. Shall we say about 10.30? We can have coffee together." She turned to Grant. "I'm ready dear. Good-night everyone, it's been a most delightful evening."

"Well, what do you think?" Julie asked, when Grant had wheeled his mother out.

"She seems a charming woman," Corynne said happily. "I'm more than ever sure about liking it here."

"That's my girl," Bill grinned. "Knew you would."

"Let's go down to the beach tomorrow afternoon. If it's this hot again it'll be the only thing to do," Julie suggested. "Bill, you're free aren't you? It's your Saturday off. We could ask Grant to come too. How about it?"

"You can ask Grant, but I doubt if he'll come," Bill sighed. "I'm all in favour. The thought of that lovely cool sea is irresistible. I wasn't built for hot weather."

When Grant came back Bill said hopefully, "How about a bathing party tomorrow afternoon, Grant? We're taking Corynne to the beach, why don't you come with us? It'd do you good to relax. You take life far too seriously these days."

"Thanks Bill, but there's a lot of business to see to while I'm here, and I shan't be down again for a couple of weeks at least. Some other time."

"The summer will be over by then," Bill growled, then stood up, stretching his massive frame. "Time we were on our way too. I need my beauty sleep."

"Must you, it's still early," Corynne protested, then glanced anxiously at Grant in case he should think she was interfering.

"Corynne's right, it is early," he agreed.

"Not for a busy doctor, old lad," Bill said. "Sorry, Grant, it's been a pleasant evening, but . . . "

Julie stood up. "Good-night, Corynne, it's been great meeting you. We'll pick you up at 2.30 is that all right?"

"Fine, I'll be looking forward to it," Corynne told her. "It's been nice meeting you too, Julie."

She followed Grant to the door, and stood waving them off.

"Good-night, Grant," she said evenly, as he closed the door and secured it. She moved towards the stairs.

"Corynne," he said sharply.

She turned.

"Mother likes you," he said. "She told me that she thinks you'll get on very well. You will stay . . . "

Corynne hesitated. "I don't know. I — haven't had time to think about it," she said cautiously, turning away.

His hand closed over her arm. "Wait, please. Listen to me," he said, and the hint of desperation in his voice surprised her.

She looked round at him, waiting to hear what he had to say.

4

GRANT let go of her arm, and took a step backwards, as though deliberately putting distance between them. His question had revived her recollections of the incident that afternoon. She had managed to push it to the back of her mind during the evening, but now the emotions came flooding back.

"I really haven't had time to make up my mind," she said. "Grant, I want to stay, but . . . "

"I know I can't have made a very good impression on you so far," he said quickly. "That business about the photographer made me look even more of an impetuous fool, but I didn't behave as badly as they tried to say."

"I didn't know you were so newsworthy," she said thoughtfully. "Bill told me you were a businessman, and spent a great deal of time in London, but for the national papers to print stories about you means that you're quite well known. The gossip columns don't bother with people who aren't."

"Notorious would be a better description," he said sadly. "It started when — Marianne died. The papers tried to make a scandal out of her death, and — someone local helped them by raking up a lot of cruel gossip. I don't know who it was, but if I ever find out . . ."

Corynne saw anger tighten his features, and a chill greyness dulled his eyes. She thought that she wouldn't like to be the cause of his anger.

"That was two years ago. Surely it's all been forgotten by now. I could understand a local paper wanting a story, but not the national papers," she said.

"Someone is making sure that the interest doesn't die. Everything I do, every little incident that I become involved with, is reported. That was why I asked Alan to meet you at the station this morning. It's no secret that you were coming here, but I didn't want you to have to face a lot of questions on your first day."

"It must make things very difficult for you," she said sympathetically.

He shrugged. "Most of the time I manage to ignore the stories, but as I do have to attend various business functions, and it is customary to take a female companion to most of them, there is a great deal of speculation as to whether my companion will become the second Mrs Grantham. I usually hire a girl from an escort agency, they can cope with the questions better, as they're not personally involved. I'd hesitate to subject a friend to the speculation."

"I would have thought you'd have spent more time here in that case," Corynne said. "At least you'd have some privacy."

"I prefer to live in London. It's more

convenient for the business for a start, and I can get lost in the crowd more easily. In London I'm just another fairly successful businessman, here in Hazelmere I seem to have become the local villain."

"It's so unfair," Corynne protested.

He smiled icily. "You know very little about me. The stories about me could be true."

"They're not, I'm sure they're not," she declared staunchly.

Her intensity made him narrow his eyes and look at her very thoughtfully.

"Your loyalty does you credit," he said, with a soft laugh. "I hope you don't find that it's misplaced."

She realized that she had been rather too forceful in his defence, and said quickly, "I'm always loyal to my employers. I've always considered that to be part of my job. In any case, I don't judge people by what other people say about them. I prefer to make my own judgements."

"Thank you for that," he said softly,

then shook his head sadly. "What you know about me so far is hardly very reassuring. And what happened this afternoon . . . "

"Let's not make too much of it," she said, meeting his shadowed eyes resolutely. "It was a momentary impulse, and these things happen to people. I'm flattered that you found me so attractive."

"Do you mean that?" He stepped closer, peering at her intently. "Corynne, do you really mean that?"

She half-expected him to declare that he was falling in love with her, and momentarily panic threatened. She'd come here to forget, and the last thing she needed was a declaration of love from her new employer.

"I'm glad that you can be so sensible about what was a natural impulse under the circumstances," he said smoothly. "The temptation will always exist, and we'd be foolish to pretend that physically we are not attracted to each other, but it's up to you — us — to ensure that we don't succumb to that temptation again. People insist on calling it 'love'," he made the word sound contemptuous, "as an excuse for their own weaknesses. It's nothing but an animal instinct that sensible people can control if they want to."

"Yes, of course," she answered with difficulty. He wanted to believe what he has said, she thought. He wanted to believe that there could be merely physical attraction involved, but why? She had to admit to a vague disappointment, but it was a relief too. She wanted no more involvement.

"I'll give you my decision in the morning," she said, and before he could respond she turned away and ran up the stairs to the privacy of her own room. She had to think. She had to decide whether to risk staying, knowing that every time she met Grant she would suffer the agony of wanting him, or leave the house immediately and never see him again.

She knew that the sensible move

would be to leave. Something told her that if she didn't, heartbreak lay ahead, but common sense was fighting a losing battle. She didn't understand what was happening, but already she had to admit that she was very disturbed by Grant Grantham's brooding presence.

She undressed and got into bed, trying to relax. The big bed was comfortable, but she tossed and turned restlessly. Sleep would not come to release her from her mental torment. She went over and over all that Grant had said. His words had been cynical, bitter, and he had denied the existence of love, yet his eyes and his body had given her a very different message.

After a while she did drift into fitful sleep, made uneasy by vague dreams, and threatening shadowy figures that seemed to be following her. When she woke it was daylight, and the birds were singing outside.

She got out of bed and padded across to the windows, throwing them wide to the morning air. It was going to be another hot day, and she remembered that Bill and Julie were taking her to the beach that afternoon, and Alan was expecting her to go to the exhibition that evening. If it had not been for her indecision she would have been looking forward to both events eagerly.

Why should she allow Grant Grantham to spoil her day? She was only here on a month's trial. Why not stick it out, and see what happens. She could have been letting a moment of madness deceive her into thinking it more than it was. In the bright light of morning she was confident that she could cope with the situation calmly and sensibly.

She washed and dressed, wondering what to do. It was early, only 7.30. and she could hear someone moving about. She went downstairs, and met Martha just coming out of one of the downstairs rooms.

"Good morning, Martha," she said, a little nervously.

"Good morning, love," Martha said, with the briefest hesitation, then suddenly she smiled broadly. "I just took Mrs G. her morning tea. Come on into the kitchen, and have one with me. Master Grant won't be down for ages, I just got to pop up with his tray, he doesn't bother with breakfast, just coffee. You can have a bit of breakfast with me if you like, unless you'd rather I served it in the dining-room."

"I'd rather have it with you, Martha." Corynne accepted the offer eagerly. "Is that Mrs Grantham's room?" She pointed to the door that Martha had come out of.

"Yes, she can't manage the stairs, poor lamb. She can shuffle round a bit, but mostly she uses the wheel-chair. Hates it she does, and her always so active."

"It must be very frustrating," Corynne agreed, following Martha into the kitchen. "It must be very lonely for her. Do any of her friends visit her?"

"She hasn't got many friends around these parts. Time was when she was always entertaining, mostly business

76

people that Mr Grantham and Master Grant brought for week-ends. The Grantham house parties were a tradition, but after the stroke she shut herself off and refused to see anyone ceptin' Doctor Hallam and Alan. Doctor Hallam persuaded her to let him bring Julie to visit, but it took a while."

"She seemed to enjoy the company yesterday evening."

"Did her good. I fancy she's taken a shine to you, love. She was on about how pleasant you was. Looking forward to having a chat with you later on."

Martha bustled around laying a tray, then picked it up and walked to the door. "Pour yourself a cuppa. I'll just take Master Grant's tray up, then I'll see about breakfast. I was goin' to bring you in a cuppa in bed, but you beat me to it."

"I was wide awake," Corynne said. "I heard someone moving around, so I came down. I don't want to put you to any trouble, Martha."

She poured herself a mug of tea, and sat at the big table sipping it. It was very pleasant in the big kitchen, with its aroma of spices and bread.

"Right. I'll just have a sup meself." Martha returned and sat down on one of the wooden chairs opposite Corynne. "Are you settling in all right? If there's anything you need, just ask."

"Everything's fine, Martha, thank you."

Martha sat sipping her tea, watching Corynne over the rim of the mug, then she said abruptly, "I shouldn't have come upstairs like I did yesterday afternoon. I hope you don't think I was snooping."

"Oh Martha, of course not. You have a perfect right to be upstairs," Corynne said awkwardly, feeling her face burning.

"Don't worry love, I wouldn't never say nothing about what goes on in the house. I hope . . . " She stopped, and looked intently into the mug. "I hope I didn't spoil nothing for you."

"There was nothing to spoil."

"Wasn't there?" Martha smiled knowingly. "I can't say as I altogether approve of the way you young people carry on nowadays, but there, it's not my place to judge. I've felt the stirrings myself on a hot day, out in the fields with my Joe." Her eyes went misty, and unfocused. "There's many a lass had to get wed in a hurry come Michaelmas."

"Martha, you don't think . . . "

"I just wanted you to know that you'll get no trouble from me, Miss. I seen things in this house that some folks would dearly love to know about, but I would never say nowt to harm the family. See no evil, hear no evil, speak no evil, specially speak no evil, that's what my Mam taught me, and that's what I do."

"Thank you Martha, you're very understanding."

Martha leaned across the table, and put a plump hand over Corynne's, squeezing it sympathetically, then she stood up.

"Now then, what would you like for breakfast. Egg and bacon?"

"I usually have just orange juice, a couple of pieces of toast, or a dish of cereal, and a mug of coffee or tea after. I really don't want a cooked breakfast."

Martha sighed. "Oh all right then. Perhaps on Sundays though. I don't come down so early Sundays, about 8.30 or so. Mrs Grantham insists on a 'lazy day', as she calls it. I take her tea in then, and she has her breakfast at 9.30. To tell you the truth, love, I don't bother to cook breakfast just for meself anyway. Mrs Grantham's like you, she only has toast, sometimes a boiled egg. Sundays is the only day she'll have cooked, so it'll suit me fine. Come and see what cereal you want, then if there's anything different you like we can order it."

After breakfast they sat chatting companionably over huge pottery mugs of strong tea, and Corynne was just wondering what she should do when the door opened and Grant walked in.

"Good morning, Martha. Good morning, Corynne," he said stiffly. "I thought I might find you here Corynne, I'd like to talk to you as soon as you've finished breakfast."

"I have finished. I'll come with you now," she said, and stood up.

"Good. We can go straight to the office then," he said briskly, and held the door open for her to go out.

He led the way into a small, but bright room a little further along the corridor. At one end there was a filing cabinet, and at the other a large desk, on which stood an electric typewriter, telephone, desk lamp, and various other items of office equipment. The windows looked out onto a small, but well-kept walled garden.

"It was originally the housekeeper's sitting-room, but Martha has her own bed-sitting-room opposite. It's more convenient for her since we shut off the upper floors," Grant explained. "I think you'll find everything you need,

I got my secretary to sort out some equipment. If there's anything she's forgotten you can get it in Hazelbury and charge it to mother."

He stood pensively running his finger along the polished top of the desk, then abruptly he jerked round and looked at her, his expression set and unfathomable.

"I hope you *have* decided to stay," he said quietly.

"Yes, I will stay, at least for the month's trial period. I like it here, and I did agree to take the position on trial. It is only fair that I honour the agreement," she answered, equally matter-of factly.

"Thank you, Corynne," he said. "You won't regret it, I promise."

He was gone, striding out of the room before she had a chance to respond, and she wandered to the window, staring out over the garden in a daze. There had been unexpected warmth in that last remark, that had totally contradicted his previous apparent indifference. What a complex man he was. Well, now she was committed to staying for a month at least.

She sat down at the desk to examine the typewriter. It was new-looking, electronic, and she recognized it as one of the latest models, and very expensive. The drawers of the desk contained everything that she could possibly need. Stationery, empty files, labels, notebooks, account books; his secretary seemed to have thought of everything.

There was an address book in one drawer, and she took it out and found that, though it too was obviously new, there were already numbers entered, most of them local; Bill Hallam's surgery, various other useful tradesmen and, as she had expected, the conference centre. She picked up the phone and dialled the number.

A brisk feminine voice answered. "Hazelcourt Conference Centre. Can I help you?"

"I'd like to speak to Mr Carey please."

"Who shall I say is calling?"

Without conscious decision she said matter-of-factly, "Corynne West. I'm Mrs Grantham's secretary."

She heard the girl say, "Alan, Mrs G's new secretary, Corynne West, wants to speak to you. Have you met her yet?" sounding muffled, as though she had covered the receiver inadequately.

She could not hear his reply, then he said clearly, "Hallo, Alan Carey here. What can I do for you, Rynne?"

"I just rang to let you know if the invitation is still open I'd like to come to the exhibition."

"Oh yes, fine," Alan said cheerfully. "I'll pick you up at seven. Tell Martha you won't be in to dinner, there's a buffet laid on. I'm sure you'll find the exhibition interesting, and you'll be able to get some idea of what goes on at the centre."

"You needn't bother to pick me up,

84

I expect you'll have a lot to see to. Grant said that I could use one of the cars in the garage, so I can find my own way."

"Well, if you're sure. I must admit I shall be pretty busy. See you at seven then. Have a good day." He accepted the offer gratefully.

Replacing the receiver she got up and went out. At the far end of the corridor was a heavy door, and when she opened it she was looking into a small garden. Until 10.30 she had nothing to do so she wandered out and along the gravel path. It led through an archway into the main gardens, and she strolled on past the hedges and flower-beds, coming out onto a larger expanse of grass, and a beautifully landscaped view.

The grounds seemed enormous, but she had only walked a little way across the grass before she came to a sharp drop, where the level of the ground fell by a couple of feet, and a low wall held the soil in place.

Suddenly she heard the thudding of hooves, and turned to see Grant, riding a magnificent chestnut horse, galloping towards her. He pulled the horse to a standstill a few yards away, and swung himself lithely from the saddle, slipping the reins over his arm.

"Admiring the view?" he called. He seemed more relaxed than he had earlier, and the riding breeches and white shirt gave him an almost cavalier appearance.

"It's beautiful," she said happily. "Does all this land belong to the house?"

He looked regretful. "It did once. Now we only own as far as the ha-ha."

"The what?"

He laughed boyishly. "The ha-ha. That wall you're standing on is called a ha-ha. It was used to separate the gardens from the grounds so that any cattle wouldn't wander close to the house. You're not familiar with the country?"

"Bristol born and bred, and proud of

it," she said, smiling. "What a lovely horse. Is he yours?"

"Yes, I board him at a local stables. His name is Rollo. Do you ride?"

"This is the closest I've ever been to a horse," she admitted, watching warily as he led the animal nearer.

"He's very good-tempered. Just don't make any sudden moves to startle him," he said reassuringly. He put a hand in his pocket and held out a couple of sugar-cubes. "Here, put them on the palm of your hand, and keep it flat. Let him know that you want to be friends."

She took the sugar nervously, and did as he said. The horse nuzzled at her hand, his muzzle warm and velvety, and she laughed at the sensation.

"It tickles."

"Yes, he's very gentle." Grant laughed. "He's got plenty of life in him though. Nothing he enjoys more than a good gallop over the moor. You must learn to ride. I'm sure you'd enjoy it."

"Is there a school near here?"

"At the centre."

"Perhaps I'll ask Alan about it this evening," she said.

"This evening?" he queried sharply.

"Alan invited me to the art exhibition at the centre. He was telling me about it on the way here yesterday."

"Alan doesn't waste time," he commented harshly.

"You don't mind, do you?" She stared at him defiantly, and he stared back angrily, then jerked round and swung himself back into the saddle.

"Why should I mind?" he said shortly, and urged the horse into a trot.

She watched him until he was out of sight, then slowly walked back to the house. If it hadn't been so unlikely she would have thought he was jealous. The more she had to do with Grant Grantham, the more unfathomable he seemed to be. His sudden changes in mood were disturbing, and his anger unpredictable.

When she got back to the house she

found Martha waiting for her.

"There you are, love. I've just taken Mrs G's morning coffee in. She's ready to see you now."

"Thanks, Martha. I've been having a wander round. Before I forget, I shan't be in to dinner. I'm going to the exhibition at the centre," she said casually, ignoring Martha's frown of dismay.

Corynne hurried into the hall cloakroom and tidied up, then tapped on the door of Mrs Grantham's room.

"Come in," Mrs Grantham called, and looked up smiling as Corynne entered.

"Do sit down, my dear. How do you like your coffee, black or white?"

"White please, but no sugar." Corynne hurried forward. She could see Mrs Grantham's hand trembling with the strain of holding the heavy silver coffee-pot, and reached out to take it. "Let me do that."

"No," Mrs Grantham said sharply, and finished pouring, handing one of the dainty bone china cups to Corynne. "I can manage quite well thank you, my dear," she smiled. "People will try to interfere, but I'd much rather they allowed me to manage things."

"I'm sorry, I'll remember that in future," Corynne apologized, sitting in the chair set opposite Mrs Grantham's.

"Do have a biscuit." The plate shook, and one of the biscuits fell to the floor as she held it out. Corynne pretended not to notice, and took one, watching nervously until the plate was safely back on the table.

"Now, my dear. Tell me all about yourself."

5

MRS GRANTHAM'S request took Corynne by surprise.

"I'm twenty-six. I worked as a nursing assistant before I trained as a secretary, and I was working as a secretary in a Bristol office before I came here," she said quickly. "My home is in Bristol, and my parents have lived there all their lives. I've travelled around quite a bit. I have two sisters, one older, one younger than me and I . . ."

"No, no, no," Mrs Grantham interrupted her, laughing musically. "I want to know what you are like as a person. Do you like music, and art? What books do you read? What are your hobbies?"

They chatted happily about books, music and sport for a while, then Mrs Grantham said thoughtfully, "Why did you decide to come here?"

Corynne met the older woman's shrewd eyes steadily. "Didn't Doctor Hallam tell you? I needed to get away from Bristol. For personal reasons . . ."

"Yes, Doctor Hallam did tell me that," Mrs Grantham nodded lopsidedly. "It's all right. I'll not pry into your personal affairs."

"I'm sorry, I wasn't hinting . . ." Corynne began, then stopped. "You're right of course. It was a man. His name was Brian Richmond. He was older than me, thirty-five, and — very much a man of the world. I was flattered by his attentions and stupid enough to believe him when he told me that I was the only girl for him. We were never engaged, or — anything."

She paused. Even now the telling was painful, but only because now she knew how foolish she had been.

"I — trusted him, and he deceived me. There were other women, and I eventually found out. He told me I was naive to have believed him, and he was right. I think I knew all the time that he couldn't be trusted, but I wanted so much to believe him. I learned my lesson, Mrs Grantham, but I felt that I needed a change and when Bill — I mean Doctor Hallam, told me about this job I thought it would be just what I needed."

"And do you still think that?"

The question was casual, but Corynne sensed a depth behind the quietly-spoken words. What did she mean?

"Oh yes," she said enthusiastically. "It's such a lovely house, and Martha has been so kind. I feel as though I belong here. I do hope you'll find me suitable."

Mrs Grantham smiled her crooked, almost malevolent smile, and again Corynne was not sure of the older woman's intention. The smile was unfortunate. It reminded her of the drawing of a witch that had once shocked her in a book, but Mrs Grantham couldn't help what the stroke had done to her facial muscles.

"At least you understand how deceitful, and — cruel, a person can be," she said bitterly. "They think I'm mad, you know. I tried to tell Grant, warn him, but he wouldn't listen. Corynne, my dear, you've got to help me. You've got to believe me . . . " She stretched out a trembling hand, and Corynne grasped it comfortingly.

"Don't upset yourself," she soothed gently. "I'll listen to you."

"Will you? Oh, my dear, promise me you'll listen to me, really listen, and — not just humour me. I feel so helpless. I have to sit here day after day and watch . . . "

"Stop it, please, Mrs Grantham. You'll make yourself ill again," Corynne urged, alarmed by the woman's obvious distress.

She remembered what Grant had said about his mother's fantasies, but somehow she couldn't accept that this woman was not in full control of her faculties. Crippled she might be, but her mind was still clear, and tormented by the knowledge that she could not share with anyone.

"Tell me what's worrying you," she urged.

"It's — a long story. You know of course that Grant was married, to a French girl called Marianne. She was a beautiful child, but wilful and wild. I sensed — wickedness in her. Grant loved her so much. Worshipped her, you could say. In his eyes she could do no wrong, but I knew better."

She let out a trembling breath and closed her eyes, leaning back against her cushions.

"Please, don't overtire yourself," Corynne warned, worried by her pallor. "Have some more coffee."

"Thank you, I will."

Mrs Grantham waited while Corynne poured another cup, and sipped at it delicately until some of the colour returned to her cheeks. Setting the cup down she struggled to lift herself higher in the chair, and Corynne helped her to get comfortable.

"When Grant was away on business Marianne — was unfaithful to him. She didn't think I knew, but I did. I tried to warn Grant, but he laughed at me. He refused to believe that she could deceive him. Just as you refused to believe it of your Brian."

"Does he believe it now?"

"I don't know. I think he must know the truth, otherwise he would not be so bitter. He'll never let me talk about her, and he gets so angry if I try. He frightens me. Someone hates him. Someone is still putting out lies about him, tormenting him. Perhaps it's Marianne's lover, whoever he is. Grant laughs at my fears. You've got to help me, please . . . "

"I'll help you," Corynne promised.

"I knew you would understand," Mrs Grantham said shakily. "You don't want to see Grant hurt either, do you?"

She was getting onto dangerous ground, Corynne thought uneasily. "No, of course I don't," she said lightly, "but I think you're worrying too much, you know. Grant's no fool, and he's quite able to take care of himself. Marianne's death was an accident, wasn't it?"

Even as she asked the question she could see that Mrs Grantham had reacted badly, and she wondered what had prompted her to ask it. Perhaps some sixth sense that warned her there was more to this story than she had been told so far.

"It was accepted as an accident, at the time," Mrs Grantham said carefully, then her expression changed, the good side of her face registering fear. "The papers — hinted at more. They tried to suggest that — she took her own life. That she was driven to it. I think Grant blames himself . . . "

"Mother . . . "

Corynne jerked to her feet as the door opened and Grant came striding in. He stopped at the sight of her, and looked at her accusingly.

"Sorry, I thought you'd have finished

your little chat by now," he said, with an icy tone in his voice. "Mother, I came to see if you wanted anything brought in. I'm just driving in to Hazelbury."

"Corynne and I are just getting to know each other," Mrs Grantham told him easily, but the fingers of her good hand toyed nervously with the folds of her skirt. "I don't want anything from Hazelbury, thank you. Corynne will be able to do all my shopping now."

"Yes, of course, that's what she's here for, I forgot," Grant retorted. "Don't tire yourself Mother, remember Bill Hallam warned you not to overdo things."

He opened the door, and looked at Corynne pointedly. Corynne took the hint. There was an unpleasant steely glint in his eyes, and she moved towards him.

"I'll come in again later, if you like," she said, glancing back at Mrs Grantham.

"Grant told me that Bill and Julie

were taking you to the beach this afternoon." Mrs Grantham gave her twisted smile. "We shall have plenty of time to talk. We'll settle your duties later, for the week-end consider yourself a guest."

"Thank you," Corynne smiled warmly, and walked out into the hall, making for the stairs.

"Wait a minute."

She felt a hard hand close over her arm, and she was jerked round forcibly to face Grant. Startled, she stood staring up into his face, and found herself responding uncomfortably to his nearness. Angrily she jerked free, and took a long step backwards, away from his all too disturbing touch.

He looked at her thoughtfully, his eyes narrowing. "What was my mother telling you?"

"We were just chatting. She asked me about my hobbies, and likes and dislikes. We're just getting to know each other."

It wasn't a direct lie, just not all

of the truth, she eased her conscience guiltily.

"I did warn you that she can be — fanciful. Please don't take anything she says too seriously, Corynne. I don't want her upsetting you."

"Why should anything that your mother tells me upset me?" she laughed lightly. "What are you afraid of, Grant? Why don't you want anyone to believe her?"

Anger flared in his eyes, and his features tightened alarmingly.

"I'm not afraid of anything my mother can tell you, but I know she can be over-dramatic," he retorted.

She said quietly, "Don't worry, Grant. I do understand your concern."

"Thank you," he half-smiled. He turned on his heel and strode towards the front door, then suddenly spun round. "Why don't you come into Hazelbury with me? It's a lovely morning for a drive."

She hesitated, remembering his previous concern about being seen with her, and he frowned.

"No obligation," he said shortly, and turned away.

"It's just that — I thought you didn't want to be seen with me," she blurted.

"I've changed my mind," he said tersely. "If you can stand the publicity so can I. There'll be gossip whatever I do."

"Then yes, I'd love to come, if you don't mind waiting while I get my bag and jacket."

"I'll bring the car round. See you out front."

She scurried away and when she went out he was waiting, leaning against a gleaming red Porsche sports car. He opened the door for her politely and made sure that she was settled, before striding round to his own seat.

"What a super car," she said huskily, clipping her seat-belt securely.

He glanced at her and laughed. "I thought you'd like it," he said. "What's the use of having money if you don't enjoy what it can buy?"

He seemed to be in an extraordinarily good mood, she thought happily. "Why don't you change your mind about coming to the beach too?" she suggested, hoping to take advantage of it. "It's a lovely day for swimming."

He gave another soft laugh. "I'll think about it," he said lightly, then glanced at her questioningly. "It's time I put the past behind me. Isn't that what you're thinking?"

"Well, yes, but what has the past got to do with . . . "

She stopped abruptly, realization dawning. "Oh dear, I'm sorry. I suppose the beach is where . . . "

"Where Marianne was drowned," he said grimly. "Yes, it is. I haven't been there since. I haven't been deliberately avoiding it, but there was no reason to go there."

"Didn't you ever take the children there?"

"The children?" He sounded almost surprised, then laughed again, this time the sound was harsh and lacking in humour. "I didn't really have much to do with the children. When Marianne died her parents asked if they could take them to live in France. I refused at first, but then mother became too ill to care for them, and it was easier to let them go. I visit them of course, but they're more French than English now, and I'm almost a stranger to them. Marianne always spoke French to them at home, and — I was never close to them."

"But — that's dreadful," Corynne said huskily. "Were you away from home a lot then?"

"Quite a lot." He spoke quietly, but there was a strange intonation in his voice. "More than I should have been, probably. Corynne, I don't want you to get the idea that I need protecting from the past. I'm not still grieving. I got over Marianne's death a long time ago. I don't need your pity."

"No, I didn't think you did," she said. "Whatever it is that's bothering you, it isn't grief. You're angry about something."

"Angry!" He repeated the word slowly. "Yes, I suppose I am angry. The past is just that as far as I'm concerned. It's over, done with, but every time a story about me appears in the papers it's raked up again, all the muck dredged up, all the rumours, and lies . . ."

His voice was rising dangerously, and he bowed his head, gripping the wheel with white-knuckled strength, obviously fighting for self-control.

Corynne sat silent, waiting for him to recover, and at length he let his hands slide onto his knees and leaned his head back against the seat, his eyes closed. He sat for a moment, then lifted his head and opened his eyes, looking round at Corynne with a rueful smile.

"Sorry, I don't often let my feelings get the better of me."

"It might be better if you did," Corynne said gently. "Bottling things up often makes them worse."

"Are you one of those women who think that men should be allowed to cry, not be taught from infancy to show the world a brave face?" he asked mockingly.

"Why not? Men can feel emotion as much as women."

"Sorry to disillusion you. I'm not the crying type," he said gruffly.

"No, you use anger instead. If you're hurt your first instinct is to hit back as hard as you can," she countered sharply. "Don't you see that it's just as dangerous as suppressing emotion altogether. Sooner or later you have to let go."

"That's quite enough amateur psychology," he growled, and reached for the ignition. "We shall be late for lunch if we don't get moving."

As they passed the gates of the conference centre she could see two coaches pulled up outside the main doors, and people milling around.

"Looks as though the centre is busy," she remarked.

"It's becoming very popular. Alan does a good job. Besides the outside groups who book it he's started regular weekly courses for riding, and various outdoor activities, with resident instructors. It keeps him out of mischief."

"Does he need keeping out of mischief?" Corynne asked, thinking that it was a rather odd thing to say.

He frowned. "That was meant to be a joke. No, of course he doesn't need keeping out of mischief. Alan is your original blue-eyed boy who never puts a foot wrong. You need help, ask Alan. His reputation is unblemished, any man with a daughter knows that she's safe with Alan. In short he's a paragon of virtue, according to the Church Ladies Committee, and believe me, their word is law around here. Do you get the picture?"

There was a distinctly ironic tone to his voice as he said it, and Corynne wondered again what was wrong between the two men. If they had once been such close friends, what could have happened to have spoiled that friendship? There was one obvious answer, but surely it was too obvious.

"Oh yes, I get the picture," she said caustically.

"So do a lot of other people," he said grimly. "One of the rumours rife at the time of Marianne's death was that Alan was a little too friendly with her when I was away on business, and oddly enough, though Alan should have been the villain of the piece, according to the stories, in fact I was the one who somehow came out in the wrong, in local opinion."

"How could that be?" Corynne asked, making the most of his unexpected frankness.

He shrugged. "They thought that I bullied her, and she turned to Alan for help in desperation. Alan has always been thought of as a gentle, kind man, and I, being a businessman, and noted for tough dealings with local traders and farmers, have always been considered hard and unfeeling. There wasn't much that I could do about it, unfortunately. I can't pretend to be something that I'm not."

"Is that why you and Alan are so touchy with each other now? Martha told me that you were really good friends once."

"Yes, we were," he said sadly. "That's part of it, I suppose."

"Isn't it about time you stopped behaving like silly kids, and talked about it?" Corynne ventured, knowing that she was taking a risk. She watched his profile anxiously, and at first it did seem that she had gone too far.

His features tightened dangerously, and his hands gripped the wheel, then relaxed again. He gave that familiar humourless rasping laugh.

"It's too late for that, Corynne. Whatever it was that triggered off the antagonism only released feelings that we must both have had for a long time."

"Wouldn't you like to be friends

again, the way you once were?"

He did not answer straight away. He glanced sideways at her, with a thoughtful frown, then concentrated on the road. She waited patiently.

After what seemed a very long silence he said tonelessly, "No, I don't think it would be possible now. We are different. We have to be."

"I didn't think you were a snob," she challenged daringly.

"I'm not," he snapped, his voice taut. "I think that's enough, Corynne. You're a stranger here, and you don't understand the situation. You can't understand it, no matter how much you think you've found out. I warned you that my mother manipulated people, and you've already let her convince you that I need help. I don't, and I will not tolerate any interference. I don't know why I've told you so much already, the events of the past have nothing to do with you."

"Not directly perhaps," she agreed quietly, refusing to let his abrupt change of manner upset her. "Indirectly they have a great deal to do with what's happening now, and what could happen in the future. You brought me here, you have to accept that I'm bound to be drawn into local affairs if I stay. What do you want of me, Grant?"

"Want of you?" he repeated the words mockingly. "I'll tell you what I want of you. I want you to run Hazelcourt House, and look after my mother. I do *not* want you trying to interfere in my personal affairs, and I do *not* want you starting some ridiculous crusade to bring Alan and me together again. Do you understand?"

"Yes, I understand," she said.

He was silent then, steering the car through the outskirts of the little town. Being a Saturday it was busy, and she looked around at the bustling shoppers.

"There's a car park just at the end of the main street," he said. "I'll meet you there at 12.30, that'll give us plenty of time to get back for lunch. I'm sorry

110

you won't have much time to wander around, but you'll be able to get some idea of what Hazelbury is like."

"I enjoyed the drive anyway," she said with a smile, as he turned into the car park and stopped, unclipping his seat-belt and getting out to hurry round and help her.

"Don't get lost," he cautioned with a grin, as they walked out into the busy street. "Martha would never forgive me if I don't get you back for lunch promptly at one."

"I won't," she promised, and watched him stride away. How confident he looked. So sure of himself, and so much in control, yet the way he had talked on the drive suggested that deep down he was very troubled, and in spite of his denials she was sure that it had something to do with Marianne, and her tragic death.

It wasn't grief, he had been right about that, but it was something even more damaging, something that still haunted him. Was Alan involved too?

She wandered down the street, looking at the shops and the people bustling around, but her mind was not on what she was seeing, only on how she could possibly help Grant come to terms with his memories. She was sure that he would never know true happiness until he did.

6

CORYNNE wandered down the busy street, looking in the shop windows. Hazelbury seemed a prosperous little town, and there were plenty of people about. The main street appeared to be very old, with quaint attractive buildings, and very little modern architecture. At one end was a market square, with a roofed stone platform in the centre, and a number of stalls around.

She paused by a newsagent's that had picture postcards on display, remembering that she had promised to let her parents know how she was settling in. She picked out a half-dozen cards for family and friends and went inside to pay.

As she stood at the counter, waiting for the woman to finish serving two elderly ladies, the headline on a

113

newspaper on the counter caught her eye:

LOCAL BUSINESSMAN IN
NEW CONTROVERSY

She started to read the story.

Is Grant Grantham the man behind the proposed new development of a leisure centre and sports complex on land adjacent to the controversial Hazelcourt Conference Centre? Local residents up in arms declare their intention to fight any move to build on prime farming land.

After last years bad harvest local farmers have been intimidated by threats of foreclosure. One farmer tells our reporter that he has been refused a development loan. There have been strange happenings, mysterious fires, and vandalism causing hundreds of pounds worth of damage to farm buildings and equipment, which has caused further financial problems for landowners in the area. Police are investigating the incidents.

"What can I do for you, Miss?"

Corynne looked up hastily. The shopkeeper was waiting to serve her.

"I'll take these cards please, and the paper."

The woman took the money she held out, and counted out change. "Young Grantham's in the news again," she remarked, pointing to the headline.

"It's scandalous, linking his name with the fires and vandalism. I don't know how much the papers can get away with printing such stories," Corynne said shortly.

She was dismayed to find that she was actually trembling. No wonder he had been so angry, if this was a sample of the kind of thing that the local papers printed about him, and obviously the local people were only too ready to believe it.

She hurried out of the shop, and strolled on. After a while she made her way back to the car park, and found Grant already in his car, quietly reading a newspaper. She tensed, preparing herself for anger. If he'd read that front page article he would surely be in a foul mood again.

To her surprise he looked up at her approach, and smiled easily.

"I hope I haven't kept you waiting," she said, hurrying the last few steps.

"No. My business didn't take as long as I'd expected." He looked at his watch. "You're right on time. Are you always this punctual?" He reached across and opened the door for her.

"I always try to be punctual," she said, clipping the seat-belt, and settling herself comfortably. She tried to hide the paper she was carrying, but he spotted it.

"Is that the local paper you've got there?" he asked.

"Yes. I — saw your name mentioned. You've seen it, I suppose?"

"I saw it yesterday morning."

So that was why he'd been in a bad

mood, she thought. "Are you planning a leisure complex?" she asked.

"No, and as far as I know neither is anyone else, but someone's put the story around and most of the locals seem to believe it."

He started up the engine and edged his way cautiously out of the car park and along the main street. Corynne saw heads turn, and fingers pointing as they passed.

"I'm surprised that the paper risked printing such a blatant accusation though. They practically made you out to be using criminal methods to force the farmers into selling," she said indignantly.

He gave the short barking laugh that she was becoming so familiar with.

"They take care not to accuse me outright. The fact that the fires and other damage were mentioned in the same article as the suggestion about a sports and leisure complex is purely coincidental. That part is probably true, there have been fires, but there always are at this time of year."

"The damage is deliberate though, if it's true. They called it vandalism."

"Yes, that is — worrying."

He sounded really concerned she thought, turning to look at him. The strain had returned, making him look older, and grim again, and she felt angry for him.

"It's so unfair," she said savagely. "Isn't there any way to put a stop to it?"

"I've tried. Legally there's nothing that can be done. I'm sure that someone local is behind it, and the paper will print any story if they think they can get away with it."

"You think — Alan might be behind it, don't you?"

"It's a possibility," he admitted, "but I don't think that Alan would be so underhanded. If he had a legitimate grievance he'd come out with it. It's probably someone I've upset without even realizing it. This sly campaign is the only way they can get back

118

at me." He sighed, then shook his head. "There'll be a retraction next week, you'll see. The rumour will be denied, but the damage is done."

She wanted to reach out to him, and put her arms round him. Her every instinct was to comfort him, but she knew that it would be foolish. He was not ready to admit that he even needed comfort, much less that she could give it.

They passed the gates of the centre, and soon he turned into the drive of the house.

"Will it be all right if I borrow one of the cars this evening to go over to the centre?" she asked.

"It would be, but there's no need. I shall be going myself, and I'll take you there and back." He switched off the engine, and turned to smile at her.

"You're going?" she said, unable to keep the surprise from her voice.

"I do own the place," he laughed lightly, and this time there was genuine humour in the sound. "I like to put in an appearance when I can."

"Sorry, but Alan didn't mention that you would be going. I assumed . . . "

"Alan didn't know," he said, and she detected a distinctly mischievous note in his voice. "Do you think he'll object?"

She didn't know what to say. It sounded as though he was teasing her, but it was so out of character.

"I wouldn't think so," she said laughingly. "He'll probably be pleased that you're taking an interest."

"I'm sure he will be," he grinned, and suddenly she saw him as the boy he had once been. If only time had not scarred him so badly. Perhaps one day he would recapture that carefree happiness, she thought hopefully.

He got out of the car and helped her out of the low front seat, and his fingers seemed to burn her arm. So close to him she looked up into his blue eyes, realizing with a shock that he seemed to be momentarily as conscious of her proximity as she was of his.

She straightened up, and for a long moment they stood, their bodies almost touching, eyes locked in silent communication, then he turned away, fumbling with his key to unlock the front door.

She followed him into the house, feeling drained, as though she had just run a race, and he turned and looked at her, his face seeming pale in the shadows.

"Thank you for the drive," she said, to break the uneasy silence. "You will come to the beach this afternoon, won't you?"

"No," he said abruptly. "No, I don't think so."

"Oh but, you said . . . "

"I've changed my mind." He was on the defensive, she realized. "I'm sorry, but — I have a lot to do, and not much time. Perhaps the next time I'm here . . . "

He spun on his heel and almost ran along the hallway and into the library. The door closed behind him decisively, leaving her staring after him in dismay.

She looked at the ornate clock. Ten minutes to one. Feeling cheated, and a little angry, she ran upstairs to freshen up before lunch.

She was first in the dining-room, and when he came in she looked at him with a feeling of loss. The grim expression had returned, and he seemed distant and unapproachable. She was beginning to find his swift changes of mood disconcerting. Just when she had thought he was mellowing, becoming more human, he had reverted to his former dark self. What could have caused the change this time?

He seemed preoccupied during the meal, and though she tried to chat, making idle comments about the town, he did not make any effort to respond. In the end she gave up the attempt, and hurried to finish and escape his brooding presence. He looked up when she pushed her plate away.

"The exhibition opens at seven," he

said. "I expect Alan told you there is a cold buffet, so we shall not be dining here. We'll leave at a quarter to seven, if that suits you?"

"Yes, that's fine," she agreed, then smiled encouragingly. "It's going to be very hot this afternoon. Are you sure you won't come to the beach?"

His mouth tightened, and he shook his head decisively. "No, I really can't spare the time. Besides — I'm not really keen on beach parties."

"You're afraid of awakening old memories," she said quietly, meeting the chill of his icy stare with more confidence than she felt. She expected him to deny it angrily, but he didn't.

"Perhaps I am," he said dully. "I don't want to be reminded of what happened, but lately it seems to be coming back to haunt me. I hate this place. I wish mother would move away but she refuses to leave. Perhaps — you could persuade her . . . "

"No," Corynne cried angrily. "I will not help you run away. You need to fight back. I don't know what it is that troubles you so much, but you can't go on like this much longer."

"Stop it, Corynne," he said dangerously, but she paid no heed to the warning in his voice.

"What is it that you want Alan to accuse you of?" she demanded wildly. "What terrible secret do you think he's holding over you?"

"How dare you speak to me like that," he shouted furiously, jumping to his feet. "You know nothing about me, or what happened here. You have no right — no right . . . "

With a visible effort he checked the furious outburst. "What are you doing to me?" He faced her, his features tight, and his eyes bleak. "You've only been here a day and already you've managed to disrupt my life. I thought I had everything under control, but now . . . "

She waited, watching the anguish twist his features, and dull the blue of his eyes to a grey misery. Suddenly the fight seemed to drain out of him.

"All right, you win," he said heavily. "I'll come to the beach. I will not let you think I'm afraid of the past, but I'm warning you, if you probe too deeply you may not like what you find."

"I'll take that risk," she told him. "Bill and Julie said they'd pick me up at 2.30. If you'll excuse me I'll go and get ready."

She went up to her room, and he was waiting in the hall when she went back down. He had changed into a casual shirt and faded jeans, and looked more relaxed. He greeted her with a boyish grin, and she responded happily. Whatever his inner thoughts he was obviously making an effort to be cheerful. Right on time they heard a noisy car chugging up the drive, and Grant opened the door, and strode out.

"Hi there." Bill descended, with difficulty, from the driving seat of the ancient and battered estate car.

"Rynne, me darling, don't tell me you persuaded old sourpuss here to come with us?"

Corynne glanced at Grant anxiously, but he was only laughing, clearly used to Bill's tactless but innocent remarks.

Grant tossed the rolled-up towel and jacket that he was carrying into the back of the car, and grinned at him. "I'm not so sure I would have if I'd known you were bringing this old wreck. It'll take us most of the afternoon to get to the beach."

"You've hurt Nellie's feelings," Bill growled, thumping back into his seat, and patting the steering-wheel affectionately. "I know old Nellie, and she knows me, she's never let me down yet. We weren't built for speed, either of us. Climb in, the pair of you, and no back seat driving."

Laughing easily Grant helped Corynne into the back seat, and got in beside her.

"Hi Corynne. Hi Grant." Julie twisted round and smiled at them

126

happily. "I'm so glad you could come Grant, I've got a picnic tea. Nothing special, just sandwiches and cakes. It'll be fun. We haven't had a beach party for ages."

"Sounds great," Grant answered lightly.

Corynne said hopefully, "For the rest of the afternoon we forget everything but having fun. Right Bill?"

"Right, Rynne." Bill let out a booming laugh, and began to sing his own version of an old song. "Oh we do like to be beside the seaside. We do like to be beside the sea. A mermaid on the rocks, and a squid to pinch your socks, oh we do like to be beside the sea."

"Bill, you're incorrigible," Corynne panted through helpless laughter. It wasn't really that funny, but somehow Bill's crazy humour was infectious. Even Grant was laughing helplessly, she saw with delight.

"That's the nicest thing anyone's said to me all day," Bill simpered, then suddenly let out a hard curse and swung the wheel sharply, as a lorry rumbled round the corner straight at them, going much too fast on the narrow road. Bill's skill saved them from a nasty accident, but the swerve took Corynne by surprise, tipping her across the seat straight into Grant's arms.

He grabbed her, and held on, and startled by the sudden emergency she let out a wild scream and clung to him frantically, expecting the car to crash. After a moment, realizing that they were still on the road, and travelling smoothly, she tried to disentangle herself, feeling rather foolish.

She distinctly felt Grant's arms tighten, preventing her from sitting up, and his eyes were looking down at her with more than normal concern. For a moment she surrendered to the ecstasy of being held against his broad chest, and feeling the warmth and hardness of his lean body. They seemed to be in a world of their own, a world where nothing mattered but being close, feeling the fiery torment of arousal, and knowing that they wanted each other.

"Are you all right?" Grant demanded, breaking the spell. For a moment longer he held her close, then relaxed his hold, and helped her sit up. His voice had a tremor, and she thought with wild joy that he had shared that moment of desire, and recognized it for what it was.

"Yes, I'm fine." She husked the words with difficulty. "That swerve took me by surprise, I'm sorry."

Grant laughed softly. "Don't be," he said, obviously trying to make light of what had happened. "It's not every day I get a pretty girl dumped in my lap."

Bill let out another of his booming laughs. "Remind me to do it again some time," he bellowed. "That crazy fool. He could have killed us all."

The incident had left them all shaken. They sat silent for a while, until Bill started up another song.

By the time they reached the coast Bill's efforts had restored the lighthearted atmosphere. He turned off the main road, and they bumped their way down a narrow lane, which finally petered out into a narrow track.

"I forgot to mention that we have to walk the rest," Bill announced with a wicked chuckle.

"What Bill means is that to get to the beach we have to scramble down a cliff path," Julie explained, collecting up a picnic basket, beach-ball, various brightly coloured canvases and a big plaited beach bag from the back of the car.

"Everyone grab something," Bill ordered. "It's not far, Rynne, and it's quite easy walking. It's worth it when we get there. Not many people come to this little bay; there's a much bigger beach with a tea place and things just a bit further along, if you want that kind of thing. We prefer this."

"Sounds much better," Corynne

agreed readily, and picked up the beach-ball and a roll of canvas.

Bill carefully locked the car and hefted the picnic basket, making a show of staggering under its weight, before lifting it effortlessly in one hand, gathering up a bundle of aluminium rods with the other, and plunging off down the track.

Grant gathered up the beach bag and few remaining odds and ends, and followed, looking as though he hadn't a care in the world. Corynne glanced round and smiled at him as he followed her, and he returned the smile warmly. Feeling a glow of happiness that she hadn't experienced for a long, long time, she followed Julie down the winding path, until they came out onto a small beach. Putting down her things she stood looking around.

They were in a small cove, bounded by low cliffs which were not much more than grass-covered hills, but which gave the cove a delightful secrecy. There was a small hut tucked back into a hollow to one side of the beach, and a tumble of large boulders, where some of the cliff-face had fallen, on the other, and that was all.

The sea was calm, rippling onto the golden sand in gentle wavelets. There was a feeling of peace and tranquillity about the place.

"It's lovely," Corynne cried, kicking off her shoes and running down to splash in the shallow water. It was warm, and she could see seashells and pebbles through the ripples.

She turned to go back to the others, and saw Grant standing staring out to sea. Then Bill yelled something at him, and he jerked, as though suddenly rousing, and moved across to where Bill was struggling with the bundle of rods and the roll of canvas. Between them they put up a small square structure.

"Here you are girls. Spare your blushes," Bill announced. "The very latest thing in bathing-huts."

Julie ran towards him, and stepped

inside, only her head and her legs from the knees down visible, then she emerged in a scanty bright green bikini. Corynne stared at her enviously. She was so slender, her breasts hardly apparent, and her waist so tiny that one of Bill's hands could almost circle it, she thought.

Corynne picked up her towel and swimsuit, and stepped inside the canvas screen. The suit was a discreet blue one-piece with high-cut sides that made her legs look longer and slimmer. There was no way of minimising the full swell of her breasts though, and she knew that against Julie's almost frail delicacy she must look substantially more solid.

She pulled open the canvas and stepped out, to find Grant standing directly in front of her. She made herself stand steady under his gaze, though remembering that he had already seen her bared to the waist there was little more for him to learn.

Their eyes met, and he smiled, then turned away and stripped off his shirt.

His jeans followed, and she saw again the lean hard body and muscular limbs, his tan accentuated by the scarlet briefs. Her breathing was oddly ragged as she watched him run down to the water's edge, thrusting into the sea until he could strike out with powerful strokes, his hair glinting golden in the hot sunshine.

She watched him swim, straight out to sea, further and further until she could barely see the bobbing dot that was his head, then she ran to the water's edge, staring out in sudden fear.

"Grant, come back," she called frantically.

"He can't hear you."

She jumped at the sound of Bill's voice. She hadn't noticed him come up behind her.

"Why are you afraid for him Rynne? What do you know?" he asked softly.

She turned. He was frowning slightly, his eyes staring past her towards that bobbing head.

"You don't really think he'd do anything as weak and stupid as to drown himself, do you?" he chided her gently. "Something's happened Rynne, and he's beginning to question things that he was afraid to question before, but whatever he finds he's not going to let it destroy him."

"How can you be so sure?" she whispered.

"I've known Grant Grantham for seven years, and I think I know what he's capable of. Marianne's death was a shock to him, but it was her life that really hurt him. You know what it's like to find that your trust in someone's been misplaced."

"Then his mother was right. Marianne was playing around with other men."

"There was more to it than that, Corynne, much more, and I don't know what it was. You're attracted to him, aren't you?"

She didn't try to deny it, she knew Bill too well to lie. "I think so Bill, but I'm not sure," she said cautiously. "It's too soon. I thought I loved Brian, but I didn't, not really."

"I should never have brought you down here." His voice was suddenly savage, and self-consuming. "Will you believe that it just didn't occur to me that you might — that he might . . . " He shook his head like some shaggy bear. "Damn it Rynne, I should have had more sense, but he's never shown any interest in women since Marianne died. At least, not the kind of interest that leads to marriage, if you know what I mean."

"He isn't showing that kind of interest now." She reached out and grasped his hand. "Bill, I don't know what he wants. I don't even know what I want, but I don't care. Don't try to interfere, promise me."

He was silent, frowning at her doubtfully.

"Please Bill. Promise."

"All right, I promise," he said reluctantly. "But remember, if you need me you only have to yell and

I'll come running." He gave her a
rib-cracking hug. "Rynne, you're a dear
sweet kid. Take care."

"I will."

She ran into the water, striking out
towards the distant bobbing head.

7

CORYNNE was not a strong swimmer. She set out with a splashy breaststroke, towards the distant dot that was Grant. Luckily the sea was calm, and she made good progress. All the same she was relieved to see Grant wave, then swim back towards her, and soon they were treading water, laughing at each other.

"I thought you were on the way to France," she called.

"I just felt like getting rid of some energy. Race you to the beach."

"No thanks, I can't swim that well." She looked round, feeling a little anxious. "I didn't realize I'd got so far out."

He swam closer. "You'll be all right, the sea's like a millpond and there aren't any dangerous currents off this part of the coast. Take your time, I'll stay with you."

She started swimming for the beach, her limbs getting heavier and heavier, and she could see him watching her as he swam lazily beside her. She was glad of his company, and confident that she was quite safe with him there, even though she felt exhausted.

"Keep going. Not far now," he encouraged, and she knew that he was aware of her struggling.

She could see the beach; it seemed only a few yards away, but it didn't seem to be getting any closer. Bill and Julie were standing in the shallows watching, and she could even see their anxious expressions, but though she put all her strength into the strokes she couldn't seem to make any progress. It was like a nightmare, the endless struggle, getting nowhere.

Suddenly she felt strong hands on her arms, and she was turned over. She felt the muscular strength of his body beneath her, and she knew that Grant had grabbed her, and was swimming with her. She relaxed, trusting herself to him absolutely.

"Good girl," he said, his lips touching her ear. Even in that waking dream of exhaustion she felt the exhilaration of naked flesh touching, and his sinuous movements arousing her to a tingling awareness of his physical attraction.

She felt herself lifted out of the water, and looked up into his face, rousing a little. The physical sensations were almost unbearable. The strong arms supporting her, and the slight roughness of hair on his broad chest, sent waves of pleasure pulsing through her. She could believe that he was carrying her to some secluded spot, where they could satisfy the passions that were consuming them. She was sure that he shared the strange, but wonderful torments that were flooding through her. She could see in his eyes the burning need. But they were not alone.

She felt him lower her gently onto the warm sand, then Bill was bending over her, frowning worriedly.

"Is she all right?"

It was Grant's voice, asking the question, and Bill stood up and stepped back, away from her.

"Just tired," he said. "Lucky you were there."

"I wouldn't have swum out if he hadn't been," Corynne said weakly. "I forgot to check how far I'd swum. Silly of me. I should have realized that Grant was a much stronger swimmer than me."

"She almost made it at that," Grant said evenly. "I could see she was tiring fast, but she stuck it out."

"She always was too stubborn for her own good," Bill growled, and Corynne sat up indignantly.

"I am not stubborn, Bill Hallam," she declared. "I didn't feel tired on the way out. It was coming back that was the problem."

"It always is," Bill chuckled. "Let

that be a lesson to you, Rynne, me old darling. Do what I do, keep one foot on the bottom, that way you never get out of your depth."

"You keep both feet on the bottom," Julie challenged. "I've never seen you do anything more than paddle. I don't believe you can swim."

"How dare you, woman," Bill bellowed. He ripped off his brightly coloured shirt, then coyly turned his back and slowly slid his trousers down, wiggling like some outrageous stripper. By the time he turned round, resplendent in knee-length shorts in a garish multi-coloured print, they were all laughing helplessly.

"Bill, you'll scare the fish," Grant chuckled, wiping his streaming eyes.

Bill ignored him, and strode down to the water, wading out up to his knees, then letting himself fall forward with an almighty splash. His arms swung in a vigorous, if rather unorthodox crawl, and looking rather like a wallowing whale he slowly swam a few yards parallel to the beach, then stood up again.

"Well?" he demanded, glaring at them.

"All right, Bill, you can swim!" Julie choked out, then ran to join him, happily splashing around in the shallows.

Corynne walked up the beach to where they had spread out their belongings, and lay down on a towel. Flat on her back, with eyes closed, she relaxed, letting the warmth of the sun ease the strain from her tired limbs.

"How much longer are you going to make me wait?" Grant said softly. "You've already proved your point."

She opened her eyes. He was sitting beside her, one leg straight out in front of him, the other bent at the knee, and his arms wrapped round it, his chin propped on the knee. He was staring at her, and there was a strange intensity in his gaze that frightened her.

She sat up. "What do you mean?"

"You're a very attractive girl. I'd like

to make love to you."

Numbed with the shock of it, she stared at him blankly.

"Isn't that what you want?" He reached out and put one hand on her knee, gently drawing it up over her thigh, until his fingers touched the edge of her swimsuit. In spite of the delightful tremors that his touch sent rippling through her, she slapped his hand away forcibly.

"What do you think you're doing?" she demanded, her voice husky and unsteady, not angry as she would have liked.

"You don't have to play hard to get to tempt me," he said, his voice low and vibrant. "You're a very attractive girl, Corynne, and you've got me in such a state that I can't think of anything else when I'm near you. Naturally I'll make it worth your while, I don't expect something for nothing."

She twisted away, and scrambled to her feet, glaring at him. "How dare you," she cried. "How dare you try to buy my favours? I knew I shouldn't have stayed, but I thought I could trust you."

He got to his feet slowly, anger building in his expression. "Damn it, what more can I say? I want you, and you know it, don't you. If you don't want money, then what do you want? Tell me your terms."

Instinctively her hand lashed out, cracking across his cheek with a force that rocked him back on his heels. He put his hand to the bruise, staring at her with such a ludicrous expression of surprise that she almost laughed, but anger won.

"How dare you offer me money," she shouted. "What kind of a girl do you take me for? You conceited, arrogant . . . "

Her voice broke, and she burst into tears, and ran off up the beach towards the path, then tripped on the loose sand, and fell, sobbing.

She felt herself lifted, and struggled wildly, until a familiar voice said gently,

"Calm down, sweetheart, tell Uncle Bill all about it."

"Oh, Bill," she subsided into his massive arms, and let her head rest on his broad shoulder, still racked by sobs. "Oh, Bill — he thought — he said . . . "

"Calm down. I'm sure there's been some misunderstanding," he soothed. "Come and have a nice cup of tea, you'll feel better. You had a fright, swimming too far, I should have realized . . . "

"It wasn't that, Bill," she choked out. The sobs had subsided to an occasional hiccupping catch of breath, but when he tried to urge her back to the beach she resisted.

"No. I can't face him, not after . . . "

"You can't run away," he said firmly. "That's not the Corynne I know. Come on, sweetheart, poor old Grant's nearly as upset as you are. I don't know what happened, but obviously you've got the wrong end of the stick . . . "

"No, I haven't." She dug her feet into

the sand, and determinedly resisted his tugging. "Bill, he's not upset, he can't be. He's more likely angry because I turned him down. He offered me money to — to . . . "

"All right. You don't have to spell it out." Bill's voice hardened. "You have to talk about it, though. It's not like Grant to — shall we say, make advances? Especially improper advances. Somewhere along the line the pair of you got your lines crossed."

Reluctantly she let him lead her back to where Grant stood, stony-faced, waiting for them a little way away from the pile of beach gear where Julie was busily unpacking the picnic basket, not looking in their direction.

"Now then, you two. What's the trouble?" Bill demanded.

Grant looked at him defiantly, then at Corynne, the icy chill in his eyes warning of his anger.

"Either I misunderstood what I took to be some rather obvious signals, or Corynne has suddenly changed her mind," he said bitterly. "I apologize if I upset you, Corynne. Obviously I was wrong. I can't imagine how I could have made such a stupid mistake."

Corynne could, and felt guilty, knowing that in a way she must have been giving him the signals that had caused the contretemps, but not for the reason he had assumed.

"Well, Rynne? is that a good enough apology for you?" Bill frowned at her inquiringly.

She wondered how much he had seen, or guessed. "Yes," she said huskily. "There has obviously been a misunderstanding."

Without meaning to she met Grant's bleak gaze, and saw momentary confusion soften the ice blue of his eyes. If only he would realize the truth, she thought desperately. Dared she try to tell him?

"Grub up," Julie called, and Bill put his massive arm round Corynne and urged her forward.

"Forget it, kid," he whispered in her

ear. "Blame it on the hot weather."

Corynne hurried into the tiny canvas shelter and put on her dress. When she emerged Julie looked at her, then at Bill, and Corynne saw him give a shrug, then Julie slipped into the shelter.

"Good idea, Corynne, I burn easily too," she called.

The mood of the afternoon had changed noticeably, and despite all Bill's efforts Grant remained quiet and moody. Corynne made an effort to be cheerful, but she felt more like running off and hiding in some secluded spot. She nibbled at sandwiches and cakes with little appetite, and after a while Julie repacked the basket.

"It's almost five," Bill announced. "Sorry to spoil the fun, boys and girls, but we have to get back. I'm on duty this evening. We must do this again some time."

Grant said nothing, but dressed swiftly and helped gather up the things. They scrambled back up the

149

path in silence, and when they reached the car Julie said casually, "I'll sit in the back with Rynne, Grant, if you don't mind."

"Suits me," he answered brusquely, and after helping load the things in, got in beside Bill without a backward glance at Corynne.

"I hope you enjoyed yourself," Julie said, settling herself beside Corynne. "You must come with us again."

"I'd like to. It's a lovely little place." Corynne tried to sound enthusiastic.

Julie chattered on idly, and Corynne tried to respond, but her mind kept going over and over Grant's incredible suggestion. She couldn't blame him, he'd been very honest about what he wanted, but how he could have believed her capable of it she dared not consider. Had she really let her feelings become so obvious? She felt a soft warm hand grasp her own, and turned, Julie was watching her, big brown eyes liquid with sympathy. There was no need for words. Julie understood.

When they reached the house Bill hurried round to help her out, and see that she had her few belongings. Grant collected his, and strode to the front door, unlocking it, and standing there waiting for her.

"Don't let it bother you too much, kid," Bill said quietly, holding her hand in a brotherly way. "He's been on edge all week-end. That beastly story in the local rag I dare say. Give him a break."

"He doesn't deserve any sympathy," she said, equally quietly, but bitterly. "He's arrogant and selfish. All that people say about him is true." She turned and walked towards the door, meeting Grant's eyes coldly, and giving a haughty little toss of her head as she went past him.

"Good-bye for now, Rynne. I'll be in touch," Julie called.

"Good-bye, Julie, and thanks," Corynne responded, then walked into the cool shadows of the hall. She heard Grant shut the door, and made straight for the stairs.

"Corynne, wait a moment, please. We need to talk . . ."

She jerked round, eyeing him coldly. "No, Mr Grantham. I don't think we have anything more to say," she told him, keeping her voice hard and calm. "You have already apologized for your insulting suggestion, and that is enough. I'll work out my month's trial as agreed, but you can start looking for a replacement now. I'll let you have my resignation, in writing, in the morning."

"Corynne, please . . ."

Was there despair in his cry, as she marched off up the stairs? She ignored it, and hurried to the privacy of her room.

After a shower she felt calmer, able to think more clearly. If Grant had made a genuine mistake, and she had to admit that she could have been partly to blame for his error, then she was being unfair in condemning him.

She faced another problem now, she remembered. She was supposed to be going with him to the conference centre. He surely wouldn't expect her to after what had happened though.

She relaxed on the bed for a while. Strange how tired she felt, but it had been a long swim. After a while, feeling rested, she roused herself to get ready for the evening. She chose a plain cornflower-blue sleeveless dress, with matching jacket, simple but smart, and applied her make-up with care.

At quarter to seven she went downstairs, and made for the kitchen. She could hear Martha clattering saucepans as she opened the door, and the mouthwatering smell of cooking greeted her.

"Martha, I'm just off to the centre," she said. "I shall need a key. I forgot to ask Mr Grantham."

"I thought he'd have given you the keys." Martha looked surprised. "You'd best take mine." She took a ring, on which there were several keys from a board on the wall. "They're all there.

The front and back doors, and the garages."

"What about the car keys?"

"Don't know nothing about them, love," Martha shrugged. "You'll have to ask Master Grant."

"Damn!"

Martha looked disapproving, then suspicious. "I thought you two would be going together. Don't make sense you using separate cars, going to the same place, unless . . . " She frowned and pretended to be intent on checking the contents of a saucepan. "I thought you two was getting along well."

"We were — we are," Corynne floundered, uncertain what to say. "I thought — if I drive myself I can leave whenever I want to. Mr Grantham might want to stay longer."

"Seems odd to me." Martha clattered the saucepan-lid aggressively.

Corynne ignored the remark. "See you in the morning, Martha. Bye for now."

"Have a nice time, love. Don't forget,

I don't start till 8.30 Sundays, but if you want tea or coffee early you can always come down and get it."

"I'll remember, thanks Martha."

She went back into the hall. It wasn't far to the centre, and Alan would see that she got back safely, she was sure. She would rather walk than have to ask Grant for the car keys. She heaved open the heavy front door, and went out.

She hadn't got far down the road when she heard a car coming up behind her fast, and stepped up onto the grass verge waiting for it to pass. Her heart leaped when she saw the gleam of the red paintwork, and then Grant was pulling up beside her.

"Get in," he said shortly.

"I'd rather walk, thank you."

"Don't be a little fool. We can still observe the niceties of polite behaviour, however we feel. It will look very odd if I let you walk to the centre."

"I forgot. You don't like people thinking badly of you, do you?" she retorted, wondering why she wanted to hurt him.

"No, I don't," he said angrily. "There's no need to be childish. You can please yourself what you do when we get there, but at least let me drive you there and bring you back safely."

He leaned across and opened the door, and after a moment's hesitation she got in, squeezing herself as far away from him as she could.

"Corynne, I made a mistake, I apologized for it. Can't you at least try to be reasonable," he said gruffly.

"I'm trying to be reasonable," she said shakily. "Can't you understand how I feel, knowing — knowing what you thought of me. It was cruel, and humiliating of you."

"I'm sorry. I assumed you were one of the new breed of independent women, who claim the freedom to seek sexual satisfaction without restrictions, the way all we men are supposed to. If I was wrong I apologize."

"You offered me payment. Trying

to buy what you wanted was — an insult."

He gave the familiar humourless laugh. "I don't believe in love, Corynne. I know that two people can be attracted to each other physically, but it's no more than a natural biological urge. I admit that I am very attracted to you physically, and I'm reasonably sure that you find me attractive. I shouldn't have assumed that you'd want to take it any further. I don't know how I can make amends, but if there is any way then . . . "

"Stop it," she cried. "You're doing it again. Trying to bribe me. Let's just forget it shall we? All right, it was a mistake, we both made a mistake, and it won't happen again. I want to go home, back to Bristol. I will work the month if you insist, but I'd rather you just forgot that agreement. You can tell your mother anything you like, say I found the place too quiet, anything, but let me go, now, before . . . "

"Before — what?" He slowed the

car, and looked round at her, his face a mask, inscrutable and hard.

"Before we both regret something we can't control." Desperation made her admit the truth. "I do find you attractive, and I think I might be stupid enough to — let you make love to me, but I know I'd regret it if I did. Let me go. While we're still able to behave sensibly."

"Work out the agreement." His voice sounded almost threatening, and she was about to protest when he added desperately, "Please, Corynne, stay for the month. If you don't, people are sure to think that I — frightened you off somehow. I pretend not to care what people say about me, but I do care. I shield behind anger, but really I want to run away and hide."

"Yes, I know that," she said dully.

"Then don't give them another excuse to condemn me. I'll stay in London. I promise I'll keep away from you, if you'll just stay. You might even — find that you don't want to leave.

You like mother, and she seems to have taken to you. Martha likes you. Then there's Bill, and Julie. What would they think . . . ?"

"Stop it," she cried. "I do understand. Give me time to think about it. I don't want to cause you any more trouble, and I don't want to upset your mother, or Martha, and they would be upset if they thought you'd — driven me away. Perhaps I've been rather too hasty . . . "

"I was trying to be practical. It was a business proposition . . . "

"I know, and that was what I objected to," she snapped bitterly. "I don't suppose you can understand that though."

"Are you suggesting that if I'd tried to rape you you wouldn't have been upset?" He didn't give her time to answer, but went on savagely. "I tried to do what I thought was the decent thing, and offer you some — reward. I could have pretended I'd fallen in love with you. Would you rather I'd simply tried to trick you?"

He paused, then said in a mocking tone, "Would you have pretended to have fallen in love with me? Would that have made it acceptable to you?"

"Hasn't it occurred to you that I might not have had to pretend?" she said despairingly.

He didn't answer immediately, but drove on a short distance, then pulled into a field gateway and stopped, twisting round to stare at her. There was a faint, mocking smile on his lips.

"So, you're going for the jackpot."

"I don't know what you mean."

He gave that unpleasant laugh. "Oh yes you do. Do you really think you're the first girl to use your charms to snare a rich husband?"

She wanted to be angry, she wanted to scream hurtful things at him, but she couldn't. She was too shocked and at the same time sorry for him.

"Is that what Marianne did?" she whispered. "Grant, no wonder you think the worst of women. She deceived you, and you think all women are as cruel as she was."

"Aren't they?" He turned back, gripping the wheel tightly, staring without seeing at the road ahead.

"No. Oh no," she cried. "I couldn't understand how you could think so badly of me, but now I do. Because of Marianne you're afraid to trust anyone."

She sat trembling, wondering what it would take to restore his faith in love. Remembering that she had experienced the same doubts herself, after Brian's betrayal.

After a few minutes silence he relaxed, and switched on the engine, backing out into the road carefully.

"Do you still want to go to the exhibition?" he asked.

"Yes."

"Right," he said, and drove on.

8

THE small car park in front of the conference centre looked almost full as Grant turned in at the gates. He drove straight into the one empty space remaining in front of the main doors, and stopped, with the car almost touching a large noticeboard that said very plainly. 'Space Reserved For Centre Bus'.

"Let's see how Alan likes a taste of his own medicine," Grant said smugly. "He's always leaving that bus right in front of the house."

"Now who's being childish," Corynne taunted him, then waited for an explosion. She didn't care if she had angered him. She was seething with resentment.

He got out of the car, striding round to open the door for her, and when she got out and started walking towards the centre he gripped her by the arm. She could hardly bear the touch of his strong fingers. They were sending tremors through her body, and she wanted to be able to hate him, with all her energy, not be reminded of the way his mere being there could send those waves of burning want coursing through her.

He jerked her round to face him, glaring down into her eyes, his own glittering steel anger at her.

"Don't call me childish," he said in a dangerously hard tone. "You're forgetting that you're an employee . . . "

"I am employed by your mother, not you," she told him, glad of another chance to vent her anger. She jerked free and stepped back, looking at him contemptuously. "And that doesn't give you the right to paw me whenever you feel like it. You may be able to frighten other people, but you don't frighten me."

She laughed, mockingly, and saw the steel in his eyes turn to molten anger.

His face seemed to tighten, his mouth compressed into a narrow line, and at last she was afraid of what she had aroused in him. This man was utterly ruthless, she thought, and she had only herself to blame for awakening the savagery that lurked under the suave exterior.

"Don't laugh at me," he hissed. "Don't ever laugh at me like that again."

Suddenly she was trembling. Unable to move, she waited for what was to come. At that moment she thought that he was capable of anything.

He reached out and gripped her by the arms, forcing her backwards into the deep shadows where the stone portico cut off the light from the hall. His grip changed, his weight holding her helpless against the chill stone of the wall. His mouth effectively checked the scream that rose to her lips, and bruised them with a brutal kiss.

Helpless she stood there, with a noisy crowd only yards away, but feeling as though she was utterly alone with this terrifying stranger. She didn't even bother to try to struggle. With her eyes shut tight she surrendered to the irresistible strength of him, knowing that even fear could not completely suppress the thrill of that strong body pressed against hers, and the exploring fingers that sent soft shudders through her.

Suddenly he let go, and stepped back, his face inscrutable in the shadows.

"What are you doing to me?" he asked savagely.

She opened her eyes, summoning all her strength, and staring at him defiantly. She had felt the want in him too. His need had communicated itself, and she was no longer afraid. He was no uncontrollable monster but a man who had momentarily succumbed to an overwhelmed passion. He was now fully in control of his actions again, though no doubt shaken by his own impetuosity, and trying to cover it by a taunt.

"I'm the one who should be asking that, not you," she told him, and in trying to cover her agitation she made her voice more accusing than she had intended.

"I'm sorry," he said, sounding as though the apology was only made with a great effort. "You're driving me crazy, damn you. For God's sake, what *do* you want from me?"

Fury drove her hand in a wild slap, so hard that it sent him reeling sideways against the wall. He leaned there for a moment, his hand to his cheek, then unexpectedly he laughed. At least, Corynne assumed it was a laugh, but it was so choked and shaky that it could have been anything.

He straightened up warily. "I asked for that, didn't I? I really am sorry, Corynne." He husked the words painfully. "Stupid of me to make the same mistake twice. I'm used to bargaining for things that I want, and it's the only way I know. Can't you try to understand that I'm trying to be honest with you? I want you, but I don't intend to pretend that I love you. Love is a myth, thought up by men to excuse their excesses, and women to explain their infidelities."

"If that's what you truly think then I pity you," she told him. "I will not bargain with you Grant. I can't be bought, I thought I'd made that clear."

"Then what other way is there to persuade you that I'm serious about wanting to make love to you?"

"I don't know," she whispered.

"You're being utterly illogical." His anger was returning. "Why can't we enjoy each other, without pretending that it's something more than physical attraction. Anything else would be pointless now. You wouldn't believe me if I told you I was in love with you, not after I've already admitted how much I want you physically, and I wouldn't want to lie to you. I respect you too much for that."

His words sent a cold chill through

her. He was right, she knew. She would find it very difficult to believe such a declaration, even if he made it. Why not accept his offer? If she loved him enough, did it really matter that he denied loving her? She asked herself the question despairingly, knowing that it did matter. It mattered so much.

"Leave me alone," she cried, and ran past him, towards the lighted doorway. Alan was standing on the porch, and he twisted round and stared at her, obviously startled by her sudden appearance out of the shadows. He looked even more startled when Grant came running after her, and jerked to a halt at the sight of him.

"What's going on?" Alan demanded, stepping forward, his fists clenched.

Grant stood his ground, glaring at him as though defying him to make a move. Corynne noticed, with dismay, that there was an angry weal across his cheek where she had struck him.

"It's all right, Alan, we were just — talking," Corynne said hastily.

"Grant offered to drive me over himself, as he was coming too."

"This is an unexpected honour, Mr Grantham," Alan said lightly. His expression stayed hard, though he let his hands fall to his sides and slowly unclenched the fists. "Come inside and meet some of your guests. I'm sure they'll be delighted to see your interest in the centre's activities."

"All right, Alan, no need for sarcasm," Grant growled, and strode past him into the reception hall, leaving Corynne looking at Alan awkwardly.

"What's the matter, Rynne? Has Grant been playing the heavy?" He frowned at her suspiciously.

Corynne's smiled waned. "We had a slight difference of opinion," she admitted. "Alan, don't interfere, please. I can take care of myself."

She saw Alan's dark eyes twinkle, then he grinned broadly. "I noticed," he said wickedly. "You pack quite a punch when you get mad."

"It was nothing," she said awkwardly.

"He'll have some explaining to do, and it serves him right," Alan declared smugly.

"You really hate him, don't you?"

"No, I don't hate him, I despise him." Alan's normally pleasant features twisted into a mask of contempt. "He isn't worth anything more. I like Hazelmere. I like running the centre. My whole life is here, and I don't intend to give all that up for one man's petty suspicions. He can't prove that I did have an affair with his wife, and I can't prove that I didn't. By mutual consent neither of us ever mentions the subject."

"Perhaps you should. If you've never discussed it how can you know what he thinks?"

"I don't want to know. I don't care. Marianne told me that she was afraid of him. He bullied her, and demanded his rights. Can you imagine it? In these times. He actually demanded his rights, like some feudal lord."

"It's hard to believe."

"You must believe it. He was brutal, Corynne. Keep away from him. For God's sake don't give him a chance to destroy you, the way he destroyed Marianne."

Corynne stared at him in shocked dismay. This was the last thing she had wanted to hear. It wasn't at all what she'd expected.

"Are you sure that Marianne was telling you the truth, Alan?"

"She had no reason to lie, as far as I know."

"Have you ever told him what she told you?"

"No."

"I think you should. He has a right to know."

"There's no point now, and anyway he'd probably deny it. Marianne isn't here to tell her side of the story. Come on, we'd better go inside, he'll wonder why we're so long."

"Let him," Corynne retorted. "Grant is your friend — was your friend. Surely you could have given him a chance to deny that accusation."

"He practically worshipped Marianne when they were first married. I couldn't understand how he could have changed so much."

"Something happened to change him. You don't like the man he is now, because you once knew a very different Grant Grantham." She hesitated, then said gently, "Alan, were you in love with Marianne?"

"Good Lord no. If she was having an affair it wasn't with me."

"Was she? Having an affair I mean?"

He shrugged. "Very probably. She was so changeable. One day all sweet and gentle, and the next wild and savage. She was so unpredictable. Grant's big mistake was in bringing her to Hazelcourt. She was bored, and she looked around for some amusement when Grant was away."

"She found it, obviously. But with whom?"

"I don't know. I don't want to know. Come on, there's nothing else that I can tell you. I shouldn't have said that much . . . "

"I won't say anything to Grant. He's going back to London in the morning, and I doubt if I shall see him very often, so you needn't worry about me."

"I am worried, but not just about you, Rynne. I feel that — we've all been waiting. Ever since Marianne drowned. It's as though she cast a spell over this place. Accusations, suspicions, and now . . . "

"Now — what?"

"I don't know." Alan turned troubled eyes to her. "Rynne, I just feel that something bad is about to happen. Don't ask me why. Ever since you arrived I've been on edge. I'm remembering things I thought I'd forgotten."

"It's strange you should feel that. Grant said something very like it too."

"It sounds crazy I know, but it's as though we were all waiting for you to make us see ourselves as you see us.

173

Things that we've taken for granted for years no longer seem so obvious."

Alan forced a laugh, and put his arm round her shoulders companionably. Just as he reached out to open the door a voice from behind made him pause, and turn.

"Good evening Alan."

Corynne saw a young man of about Alan's age. He was tall, but thin and rather stoop-shouldered. His gold-framed glasses reflected the light from the hall, blanking out his eyes and his face seemed almost featureless. He was smiling as he approached them.

"Hallo Roger," Alan greeted him cheerfully. "So you managed to get here. How's Joanne?"

"Not too well I'm afraid, that's why I didn't bring her." Roger sighed. "You seem to have quite a good crowd. I had a job to find a parking space, and then I had to go right round to the backyard. I wouldn't have thought an art exhibition would have attracted so many people."

Alan laughed. "Free food, and wine, and no competition. There's no social in the church hall tonight."

He turned to Corynne. "Corynne, let me introduce Roger Sallen, local schoolmaster, church organist, cub master, member of the local parish council, and pillar of local society. Roger, meet Corynne West, Mrs Grantham's new secretary."

"I'm very pleased to meet you," Sallen said politely. "Shall we go inside," Alan suggested, pulling open the swing-doors.

A wave of heat, and smells of food and hot humanity enveloped Corynne as she walked into the crowded foyer. Alan introduced her to various local people, who greeted her pleasantly enough, though she was very conscious of their scrutiny, and the whispers that passed among them as she moved on.

Alan guided her round the centre, pointing out various lecture rooms and games rooms on the way, until they emerged onto a broad wooden veranda. There were small tables and comfortable chairs all along it, most of them already occupied. Floodlights illuminated a colourful garden, where sunbeds and garden chairs were set around a lawn, for guests to sunbathe during the day. A high yew hedge surrounded the area, sheltering it from the wind.

"Come on, let me show you the lake by moonlight," Alan said wickedly, putting a hand under her elbow and urging her down the gravel path that flanked the lawn, through a gap in the hedge, and out into a much less formal area.

Here the grass was coarser, and the path wound picturesquely between shrubberies, with a surprise round every corner. Sometimes it was a statue, sometimes a colourful bush, and once a delightful little vine-covered rustic arbour. Soon they came out on the grassy banks of what was really little more than a large pond.

"We call it a lake, it sounds better

in the brochures," Alan said with a chuckle.

"It's a very attractive place," Corynne said, looking round appreciatively. "It all looks beautifully well-kept, Alan. You do a good job here."

"Thanks." Alan smiled down at her, his dark eyes accentuated by the silvery light.

For a moment she thought he meant to kiss her, and was about to move out of his reach, when she heard the crunch of footsteps. They had a somehow aggressive sound, and Alan put a protective arm round her.

She watched as a shadowy figure strode round the last bend in the path, and emerged into the comparative light of the more open lake-side.

She was more angered than surprised to see that the newcomer was Grant. She felt Alan's fingers tighten on her shoulder, and instinctively tried to pull free, then defiantly pressed more closely into the curve of his sheltering arm.

"I thought I might find you here."

Grant's voice was quiet, but chill. "Alan, I'm leaving. Bring Corynne back to Hazelcourt safely, will you?"

"Yes of course," Alan agreed. "I hope you approve of what you've seen this evening, Grant?"

It could have been intended as a taunt, Corynne wasn't sure, but Grant took a step closer, and in the cold light his features seemed carved out of stone.

"You seem to be doing a very good job," he said evenly, but again there was a steely tone to his voice. He stood there stiffly, staring at Alan, then abruptly turned on his heel and strode away.

As his crunching footsteps receded into the distance Alan let out his breath in a long sigh.

"If I wasn't so sure it was impossible, I'd say Grant was jealous," he said doubtfully.

"How can he be? He has nothing to be jealous about."

Alan's arm tightened round her

shoulders. "Come along, let's go back to the hall. They'll have started dancing by now," he said brusquely, and she got the feeling that he didn't want to risk anyone misconstruing their absence.

As they approached the lawn they could hear some kind of uproar going on, voices raised, and Alan broke into a run.

"What the devil is going on?" he panted as they got closer, and saw a crowd milling around on the lawn.

"Oh Alan, someone seems to have had a fall," Corynne cried.

She felt a sudden dread grip her as Alan pushed his way through the crowd, and she followed. In horror she stared down at the figure sprawled there on the grass. It was Grant. Blood was seeping through his hair, and trickling down the side of his face. His eyes were closed, and he seemed to be scarcely breathing.

Alan took charge. "Has anyone phoned for an ambulance?" he demanded, and when the answer was negative despatched one of the men to do so.

"Does anyone know what happened?"

A frightened looking boy stepped forward. "I saw him come staggering out of the bushes. He took a couple of steps then folded up. We thought he'd had a heart attack or something, then — I saw the blood . . . "

He turned away, his hand to his mouth.

"Jeff," Alan called to a young man in a white jacket, who was obviously one of his staff. "Get that youngster inside, and take him to my office. You'd better call the police."

"Police?" Corynne croaked. "Alan, you don't think . . . "

"Someone tried to kill Grant." Alan's face looked pale in the harsh floodlights. "They damned nearly succeeded." He stripped off his dinner-jacket and covered Grant with it.

"Is he going to be all right . . . ?"

Corynne dropped to her knees beside the limp form, foolishly reaching out to touch the blood soaked hair.

Alan caught her wrist. "Go inside, Corynne," he said sharply. "Find Pat Marsh, my assistant, she'll probably be at the reception desk. Tell her what's happened, and ask her to phone Bill Hallam. They'll take Grant in to Hazelbury General, and I'd like Bill to be there. Can you do that?"

"Yes, yes of course, but . . . "

"There's nothing you can do here. The ambulance will arrive any minute. I'll go with him."

"Alan, who could have hated him that much?"

"Robbery could have been the motive, we shan't know unless — until Grant himself can tell us exactly what happened. Now do as I asked you, please."

He stood up and lifted her to her feet, giving her a push to start her walking. In a daze she stumbled into the building, and found her way to the reception hall.

9

A DARK-HAIRED young woman was sitting behind the reception desk, and Corynne ran to her in a daze.

"Pat. Are you Pat Marsh?" she asked shakily. "Alan sent me. There's been an accident."

"I know. Come into the office."

Pat caught her by the arm and led her through a door behind the desk into a small room lined with filing cabinets and cupboards, with a couple of small but comfortable-looking armchairs, and a desk at one end.

"Sit down." Pat pushed Corynne into one of the armchairs, and went to the small sink unit and tea-making facility in one corner.

"You look as though you've had a shock. I'll make you a cup of tea. It's all right, the ambulance is on its way."

"Alan wants you to ring Doctor Hallam and tell him that Grant's being taken to Hazelbury General."

"Oh no! Was it Mr Grantham who had the accident?" Pat stared at her in dismay, then whirled round and grabbed for the phone on the desk.

Corynne listened as she briskly gave the message, then closed her eyes and leaned back in the chair limply, dazed by the shock of what had happened.

A steaming mug was thrust into her hands. "Here, perhaps this will help," Pat said.

Corynne looked up. "Thank you," she whispered. "I'm sorry. I don't usually go to pieces like that, it was seeing him lying there, covered in blood . . . "

"Just take it easy. You must have had a nasty shock," Pat quickly cut her short. "Was he really attacked?"

"I don't know for sure, but Alan seemed to think . . . " Her voice broke.

"I know he isn't very popular, but I

can't imagine anyone wanting to hurt him. Not really injure him I mean," Pat mused. "Is Alan going to the hospital with him?"

"Yes."

"Would you like to arrange for someone to take you back to Hazelcourt? I suppose we should let his mother know . . ."

"No, not yet, not until we know more," Corynne said quickly. "It might only worry her unnecessarily. I'm fine now. I'd like to stay until Alan gets back, if that's all right?"

"Yes, of course. Make yourself comfortable. I must get back to the desk, but just yell if you want me. There's plenty of tea in the pot, help yourself," Pat said sympathetically.

Pat went out, and Corynne was left alone with her thoughts, but not for long. Pat kept popping in to check that she was all right, and eventually sank into the second chair with a sigh of relief.

"Desk's closed for the night, thank

goodness," she said. "I can relax now."

"Is there any news?"

"No, I'd have told you right away. Don't worry, I'm sure he'll be fine. He's in very good hands."

"Who could have hated him enough to try to kill him?" Corynne whispered. "Oh, Pat, it scares me to think that someone could be so vicious. His mother insisted that he was in danger, but he wouldn't listen to her. She said there'd been other incidents . . . "

"Nothing like this," Pat said thoughtfully. "He's had a couple of near-misses. A chunk of masonry fell off the church tower and just missed him once, and the girth on his saddle broke when he was galloping Rollo, and he had a nasty fall. He insisted that it was just worn, but Steve Parker, the riding instructor, said it looked more as though it'd been cut. Grant wouldn't do anything about it though."

"Perhaps he knows who was responsible."

Pat shook her head. "He'd be a fool

185

to keep quiet if he does. If someone
tried to kill me I wouldn't keep quiet
about it, would you?"

"No, but he might have a good
reason."

"It'd have to be good then. I can't
imagine . . . "

Pat broke off and jumped up to
open the door as footsteps sounded
outside.

"Alan," she said eagerly, as he strode
in. "Any news?"

Corynne got to her feet slowly, trying
to read from his expression before he
got as far as speaking. He looked
strained and worried, but not too grim.

"Bill's pretty sure that he's going to
be all right." He spoke the words she
wanted to hear quickly, and smiled
a little. "He regained consciousness
in the ambulance, and the injuries
were mostly superficial scalp wounds.
He looked worse than he was. Bill's
keeping him in for observation, he has
a mild concussion."

"Thank God," Corynne breathed

huskily. "Does he know who attacked him?"

"He says he was hit from behind, and didn't see anyone. The police are checking, Rynne, but there isn't much to go on. They think it was probably someone local, who knew that Grant would be here tonight, and took the opportunity that presented itself."

"No one did know he was coming, did they?"

Alan frowned. "That's right. He didn't even let me know."

"That means that it was someone at the exhibition tonight."

"Most of the locals were there," Alan shrugged. "It doesn't help much, but I'll tell Inspector Phillips anyway. I'd better take you back to Hazelcourt. You must be worn out. Have you said anything to Mrs Grantham yet?"

"No, I thought it better not to until there was some more definite news."

"Good girl. Pat, don't wait up for me. I shan't be long, and I'll make the final check. I think everyone's in bed at last."

It was eerie walking through the darkened building, and Corynne was glad when they reached the car park, and Alan guided her to a rather battered blue saloon and helped her in.

"He really is going to be all right, isn't he?" she asked, as he drove out through the gates. "You weren't just saying that?"

"I assure you, I have it on Bill's authority. Why are you so concerned? I thought you and Grant were at daggers drawn."

"So did I, Alan. Only I realized that it wasn't true. I am concerned about him."

Alan was silent until they reached the gates to Hazelcourt House. He turned in, and pulled up at the doors. As Corynne unclipped her seat-belt and reached for the door he caught hold of her wrist.

"Rynne, listen to me, please. You had a shock and you feel sorry because

Grant got hurt, but don't let it cloud your judgement. He's still the same old Grant."

"I know, but I can't help how I feel. I love him, Alan. I didn't want it to happen, but it has."

"Rynne, I don't know what to say," Alan sighed wearily. "Whoever attacked Grant tonight must have had a damned good reason, and he is going to have to do something about it. That's why I called the police in. Even Grant admits that something has to be done. He had a nasty shock tonight, and I think he's realized that the past is catching up on him."

"What past? What do you mean?"

"Did you know that there was a rumour that Grant killed Marianne, or at least drove her to take her own life?"

"It's not true."

"True or not, I think someone believes it. That someone is the man who was Marianne's secret lover."

"Of course. He wants revenge. Oh

Alan, what are we going to do?"

"*You* are going to bed. Tell Mrs Grantham in the morning that Grant's had an accident, he's in hospital, but he's not badly hurt, nothing more, do you understand? That's what he wants."

"Yes, I understand."

"Good. Bill's coming over in the morning to see her, and reassure her. He'll tell her as much as he thinks wise."

"She'll suspect. She's convinced that someone's been trying to kill him."

"I know. There isn't much we can do about it for the moment. She happens to be right, though Grant did his best to persuade her that it wasn't true. He didn't want her to worry."

He got out of the car and opened the door for her. "We'd better go round to the back and wake Martha."

"There's no need, I've got the keys."

Corynne found the bunch and handed it to him. He opened the door, and stood back to let her go in.

"I'll come over in the morning and see if everything's all right. Inspector Phillips will want a word with you, but I told him you were with me, and that we arrived after it all happened." He gave her back the keys and turned away. "Good-night, Rynne."

"Good-night, Alan, and thank you for your help." She shut the heavy door as quietly as she could, and drew the bolts. Wearily she climbed the stairs, and prepared for bed.

Sleep would not come for a long time, and she twisted and turned, as her mind relentlessly recalled the bitter moments of resentment. She now knew them for what they were. The result of love, spurned and twisted by a man who was not capable of love himself. Would he ever realize his mistake? Would he ever be able to drive out the shadows of a past that would not let him forget his hurt?

Corynne woke to a grey morning. Still feeling weary she got out of bed, washed and dressed, and shuffled downstairs to the kitchen. Martha was just putting the kettle on.

"Oh lovey, whatever is the matter? Are you ill?" Martha exclaimed, bustling towards her, her usually cheerful face anxious.

"Grant had an accident last night. He's in hospital," she blurted out.

"What kind of an accident? Here, come and sit down."

Martha managed to ease her into a chair, make the tea, and pour a steaming mugful in what seemed only a moment, and Corynne sipped at it gratefully. She welcomed Martha's motherly concern, it was just what she needed. She told Martha all that she knew.

"How bad is he?" Martha demanded.

"Bill says he's going to be all right. He's got a mild concussion. They kept him in overnight for observation."

"Well, that doesn't sound too bad." Martha heaved a sigh of relief. "The look of you I thought he was at death's door."

"Mrs Grantham doesn't know yet. Doctor Hallam is coming over to see her later this morning, and I must tell her what happened first. I hope it doesn't upset her too much."

"She's always worried about Master Grant, when he's here. He won't have it, but she's right enough. Someone's got it in for him. It's time something was done."

"Alan called the police."

"Good for Alan," Martha said firmly. "I'll just take Mrs G. her tea." She bustled out with a tray and was soon back. "I'll be getting on with breakfast. You can tell her after she's eaten, otherwise she wouldn't touch a bite, I know her," she said flatly. "Master Grant always popped in to see her first thing, soon as he was up, and she'll soon start wondering what's wrong. You'd best have something too, keep your strength up."

"I don't want anything to eat, thanks."

"You'll have a good breakfast and

like it," Martha told her, in a tone that brooked no argument.

Corynne did her best to eat the eggs, bacon and tomatoes that Martha set before her, with slices of yeasty farmhouse bread. With her plate only half-cleared she pushed it away.

"Sorry Martha, it was very nice, but I'm really not very hungry. I'll go and tell Mrs Grantham now before she has time to start worrying."

She hurried along to Mrs Grantham's room, and tapped on the door nervously.

Her 'come in' sounded tense, and Corynne knew that she must already have guessed that something was wrong.

"Grant had a bit of an accident last night," she said quickly, as soon as she was inside. "He's not hurt badly, nothing to worry about, but Doctor Hallam has him kept at the hospital overnight for observation. Alan is coming in to see you this morning, and he'll explain, and Doctor Hallam will be calling later."

"And I'm not supposed to worry."

Mrs Grantham sighed gustily. "Don't they realize that all this secrecy only makes me worry more."

"I'm sorry . . . "

Mrs Grantham smiled and held out her good hand. "It's not your fault, my dear, I didn't mean to sound as though I was grumbling at you. I'm sure you're only doing what Doctor Hallam told you to do. Come and sit down, and tell me just what happened. Please, don't treat me like a foolish, fanciful old woman. It wasn't an accident was it?"

"No, I don't think it was," Corynne said. In spite of both Alan and Bill's caution she was sure that Mrs Grantham should know the truth. Quickly she told the older woman everything that she knew about what had happened. Mrs Grantham listened quietly, and when Corynne had finished she nodded with a satisfied expression on her twisted face.

"So this time the police were called in. I'm sure that Grant will be angry with Alan for doing that, but he was right. It's time this person was stopped."

There was a rap on the door, and Martha came in at Mrs Grantham's summons.

"Sorry to interrupt but there's an Inspector Phillips here, asking to speak to Miss West."

Corynne stood up. "Thank you, Martha. Will you tell him that I'll be right out." She waited until Martha had closed the door behind her, then said gently, "Try not to worry any more, Mrs Grantham. You were right all the time, but Grant didn't want you to worry."

Mrs Grantham smiled her wry twisted smile, and somehow it seemed appropriate. "I know that my dear, but thank you for believing me. I do hope that all this unpleasantness will not drive you away from Hazelcourt."

The words brought back all Corynne's doubts about her situation, but she said lightly, "I'm here for a month at least. Now please try to rest, or I shall have

Bill Hallam after me."

She left Mrs Grantham laughing, and went out. A tall, bulky man was strolling idly up and down the hall, studying the family portraits. He turned around at her approach and smiled in a friendly way. He was middle-aged and gave Corynne a feeling of reassurance.

"Inspector Phillips. I'm sorry to keep you waiting," she said. "Come into my office."

She led the way, and Phillips followed settling his bulk comfortably on one of the chairs.

"Well, Miss West. What can you tell me about the attack on Mr Grantham?" he began without preamble.

"Not much," Corynne said regretfully. "I was with Mr Carey, and we didn't see anything until it was all over. Mr Grant was lying on the lawn unconscious when we got there."

"I see." Phillips nodded and asked a few more casual-sounding questions about who they had seen, and if she had any ideas. She found herself talking to him a little more freely than she had intended, and he listened with interest, occasionally writing something in his notebook.

She ended by saying regretfully, "I'm sorry I haven't been much help Inspector."

"On the contrary," he smiled and stood up. "You have been very helpful Miss West."

She saw him out, and as he was driving away Bill Hallam's shabby car turned in at the gates. She waited for him.

"How is he?" she demanded, as soon as he got out of his car.

Bill bounded up the steps, grinning broadly, and strode into the hall. "He's fine, Rynne me darling. Did you get any sleep last night?"

"Not a lot," she admitted, closing the door. "Do you want to go straight in to Mrs Grantham?"

"No, I want to have a word with you. What's all this nonsense about you falling in love with Grant? Alan told me how upset you were last night. I thought you'd decided he was an utter swine, and . . . "

"Don't you start, Bill Hallam," she cried furiously. "I was wrong, that's all, and anyway it's my business how I feel about him. Alan had no right to tell you . . . "

Her voice faded off into a wail, and she collapsed into the shelter of Bill's massive arms, weeping helplessly. He held her until stress and anger were washed away, and she nestled quietly in his fatherly embrace, the tears spent.

"Feel better now?" he asked gently. "Alan wasn't gossiping you know, he's concerned about you, and he doesn't want to see you getting hurt, any more than I do."

"Oh, Bill, I'm so confused . . . "

"I know. Now you pop upstairs and put your face straight, while I go and have a chat to Mrs Grantham. You have told her that Grant had an accident, haven't you?"

"She knows it wasn't," Corynne

said shakily. "I'm sorry, Bill, but she wouldn't believe me. In the end I thought it was better to tell her the truth. She took it rather well."

"Fine, then I'll just pop in and reassure her. Give you all the details later."

Bill let her go and shambled off, and Corynne fled upstairs to repair the ravages her tears had caused. When she got back down Bill was nowhere to be seen, and she tried the kitchen. Sure enough he was there seated at the table, munching a large slice of cake, and holding a steaming mug of tea.

"I was just telling Martha that Grant will be home some time this afternoon. Alan's fetching him," he told her through a mouthful. "He'll have to take it easy for a couple of days, but apart from a nasty headache he's fine."

He munched another mouthful and swallowed, then looked at Corynne with a wicked smile. "Except for his temper there's no harm done. He's had orders to rest so Martha will be taking his meals up to his room."

"That I will," Martha said happily. "I'll make him some of my beef broth. Always made him beef broth when he was sick as a child."

"That's right, Martha, you coddle him." Bill finished the cake and stood up. "Must go. Thanks for the cake and tea, Martha. I never could resist your cooking."

Corynne followed him out to the front door, and he paused on the top step, frowning at her thoughtfully.

"Watch your step with Grant, Rynne. He's touchy to say the least, and the best thing you can do is to leave him alone. Let him make the first move. Are you listening to Uncle Bill?"

"I'm listening."

"Grant will be able to go back to London by Monday or Tuesday, and then you'll have a chance to think about things a bit more objectively. Do be careful. You've only just got over one mistake, don't jump right into another."

"Bill, I know you mean well, and I'm grateful. I will think carefully about — everything, I promise. In any case I don't think how I feel will make much difference, unless something happens to make Grant do some thinking too. He's so bitter and twisted right now."

"Something has happened, Rynne," Bill frowned. "He's accepted the fact that he needs help. He always refused to have the police brought in, but Alan had the courage to risk his anger last night. Oh Grant was angry all right, but it's out of his hands now."

"I wondered — if he thought Alan was behind all the persecution. He said he didn't, but it's the only thing that makes sense."

"If you call it sense, to ignore a threat on your life," Bill said caustically. "Yes, I think he did have a sneaking suspicion that it might be Alan, but he didn't want to believe it. Alan always was the obvious suspect. He saw a lot of

Marianne when Grant was away. From being too trusting, Grant's now become suspicious of everyone."

"Will he ever be able to forget Marianne's deceit?" Corynne asked miserably.

"I wish I could say yes, Rynne, but I can't. Some people can get over such a trauma, you did, but with Grant the hurt has gone deep. Perhaps part of the trouble is that he feels guilty. He feels that he was to blame for what happened — her death — Alan's estrangement. In a way perhaps he was."

"I don't believe that. Oh Bill, there must be some way to help him . . . "

"Don't count on it, sweetheart," Bill shrugged. "He's a stubborn man, and anger is the only defence he's got left. The healing has to come from inside him. I've done all I can, it's up to him now."

"Sometimes it is easier not to trust anyone. That way you can't get hurt again," Corynne said huskily.

"Chin up, sweetheart. At least you understand what Grant's been going through. Just don't expect too much. You may have to settle for less than you'd like."

"I can't, I won't," Corynne declared wildly.

"Then be prepared for a long siege," Bill laughed sympathetically. "If you should want me just ring the surgery. There'll be someone to take a message If I'm not there. Keep an eye on him, but he should be O.K."

"Thanks Bill."

She watched him drive away, then slowly walked back into the house.

10

IT was already almost lunch-time, and Corynne had little appetite. Martha was preparing their meal, a light salad with thick slices of juicy farm-cured ham, and home-made pickle, and she struggled to eat with little enthusiasm. She refused the apple tart that Martha tried to tempt her with, and pushed her plate away.

"Sorry Martha. I'm just not hungry. If you'll excuse me I think I'll go up and have a rest. I didn't sleep very well last night."

"You do that, love," Martha nodded agreeably.

Corynne escaped to her room, stretched out on the bed and closed her eyes. The next thing she knew was a gentle tapping on the door, and Alan's voice calling.

"Corynne. Are you there?"

She sat up, trying to collect her thoughts, dazed by sleep, then remembered that he had been bringing Grant home.

"Coming," she called, and swung her legs off the bed, trying to smooth out the creases in her dress and tidy her hair as she went to open the door.

Alan was smiling cheerfully. "Grant would like to talk to you. He's in his room. Bill ordered him to stay in bed and rest, but he insists that he can't rest until he's talked to you. Will you come?"

"Of course I'll come. Alan — you look as though something great has happened."

"We've talked too, Grant and I, and — it's all getting sorted out now, Rynne. Thanks to you."

"What did I do?"

"You started us both thinking. You saw it all from a different point of view, and you weren't afraid to tell us what *you* thought. Don't expect too much, there hasn't been a miracle or

206

anything dramatic, but at least we're talking about things that we've both been afraid to talk about before."

"About — Marianne?"

"Yes, about Marianne, and a lot of other things that we've both been bottling up. It'll take time, but we've made a start."

"Alan, that's great news."

"Don't raise your hopes too high, Rynne." Alan's expression sobered a little. "It's early days, and Grant still has a lot of thinking to do. He isn't going to change overnight."

"I understand, and thank you, Alan. Give me five minutes to freshen up, and I'll be with you."

She closed the door on him and ran to the wardrobe, rattling the few dresses along the rails, urgently trying to find something that she felt would be suitable. Not too revealing, but not too severe either. Finally she settled on a light summer dress in a soft blue linen-look fabric with a full skirt and fitted waist. It was pretty, but at the same time business-like, the kind of thing she would wear to the office. A quick splash of cold water to freshen her face and make her skin glow, a comb through her tangled hair, and a touch of lipstick, and she felt ready to face Grant.

Alan was wandering up and down the corridor when she emerged, and she saw his smile widen.

"You look very nice," he said, and the compliment boosted her confidence considerably. Feeling unaccountably nervous she waited while he opened the door of Grant's room, and then followed him in.

The first shock was to see Grant in bed, in black silk pyjamas that accentuated his pallor. The dressing on the back of his head brought home the realization of his narrow escape, and she forgot caution and ran to the bed.

"Grant, you look awful," she cried, shocked into tactlessness.

He laughed softly. "Thanks for the

reassurance," he said lightly. "Sit down, I want to talk to you."

He indicated the chair set beside the bed, and she sank into it, not taking her eyes off his face. He looked tired, and there was no doubt that he had had a nasty shock. Pain shadowed his eyes, and his features were set and drawn.

"How are you feeling?" she asked.

"Shaky." He gave that familiar humourless laugh.

"I'll leave you to it," Alan said. "I have a lot to do at the centre. See you later."

"Thanks, Alan," Grant said quickly. "Thanks for everything."

Alan nodded, and went out, closing the door quietly.

There was a long silence while Grant and Corynne looked at each other intently, then Grant said gruffly, "I want to apologize for my outrageous suggestions to you, Corynne. My only excuse is — that I was afraid of letting you think that I might be becoming — emotionally involved with you."

"I understand," she told him, determined not to let him anger her this time.

He looked uncertain, as though he thought her quiet acceptance too easy. "I wonder if you do understand," he said doubtfully. "I find you very attractive, I'm not denying that. The problem is that I couldn't think of any other way to — to — make you understand what I wanted."

"You made it very clear what you wanted," she said evenly.

She saw him wince, and knew that her words had struck home.

"Corynne, I told you I don't believe in love," he went on, his voice becoming more agitated. "I don't know how to approach you."

"You're a fool if you think that any decent woman would let herself be bought. I consider that an insult," she said bitterly.

His fingers pleated the silk sheet restlessly. "I said I'm sorry. What more can I do?"

"You've done enough. Find some other woman to . . . "

He cut her short. "I don't want another woman, I want you."

"What?" she gasped, his quiet interruption deflating her anger.

"I said I want *you*. I'm asking you to marry me."

She was silent, staring at him in a daze. It was so unexpected.

"I want you to be my wife," he said quietly. "You're everything I admire in a woman. You find me physically attractive, and there should be no problems about that side of the partnership. I'll have my solicitor draw up an agreement, and we can discuss terms that will be to our mutual satisfaction. What do you say?"

"No!" she screamed wildly. "No! No! No! You don't know me at all. I love you, Grant, and I don't want a marriage of convenience. Unless you can tell me honestly that you love me, you can forget it. I will not settle for a business arrangement."

She fled from the room, not waiting to see his reaction. Suddenly she had to get out. She couldn't bear to be cooped up under the same roof as Grant any longer. She ran down the stairs, and through to the office, where she had left her handbag, then had an idea.

She jerked open the desk drawers and hunted through them, and sure enough in one of them there was a bunch of keys. They were all there, neatly labelled, front and back doors, garages, and car keys. She unhooked the car keys and ran out, hoping that she wouldn't meet Martha. She didn't feel like explanations.

Her luck held. In the garage she found a blue Cortina, and a white Mini. She chose the Cortina, and edged it out cautiously. She had no idea where she was going. When she reached the conference centre gates she slowed, meaning to turn in, then changed her mind and drove on. Soon she was in the village, and she turned into the tiny car park on the main street, and got out of the car.

It was very quiet. A few people, obviously visitors, were wandering around the picturesque cottages and peering in the windows of the shops. Several of them were open. A gift shop, and a little cafe advertising home-made cakes and cream teas, seemed to be doing a brisk trade. The centre had certainly brought prosperity to the village, Corynne thought.

Just down a lane she could see the old thatched lych-gate of the church, and she strolled down and went through. The heavy carved door of the church stood ajar, and she slipped through the gap into the cool quiet interior.

She felt a sense of tranquillity as she walked silently down the aisle towards the altar. There were flowers everywhere, and a faint smell of polish. The thick walls muted any outside noises, and she let the peaceful atmosphere soothe her troubled thoughts.

Sunlight glittered in varicoloured

fragments through a lovely stained glass window, and it was obvious that the church, though small, was well cared for.

"Good afternoon," a gentle voice said, and she turned to find a very old man smiling at her. He was just coming out of a small doorway behind the choir stalls.

He had a saintly look, she thought, his white hair almost a halo round his seamed features. He was tall, and must have once been a fine figure of a man, but now age had wasted his flesh, and his clothes hung on a skeletal frame.

"Good afternoon," she responded. "Are you the minister?"

He sighed. "I was once, but now I am merely a visitor, like you. Allow me to introduce myself. Bertram Sallen."

Corynne took the withered hand that he held out, feeling it like dry twigs in her grasp. "I'm Corynne West. I met a young man named Roger Sallen at the conference centre last night. Is he a relative of yours?"

"Indeed, he is my son."

"It's a very beautiful little church," she commented. "What a magnificent window for a small country parish."

"Donated by the Grantham family." He smiled a little. "As were the candlesticks, and altar goblets, the bell, the reredos . . . " He stopped for breath, chuckling to himself rustily. "The village owes a great deal to the Grantham family."

"They don't seem to appreciate what the present Grantham has done for them," Corynne remarked rather spitefully, and regretted it when the old man sighed heavily.

"I have known the Grantham family for a long time, my dear. I have not always approved of what he does, either."

His remark surprised Corynne, and something impelled her to ask, "Did you know Grant's wife, Marianne?"

To her horror the old man stiffened, and his hand fluttered across his chest in the unmistakable sign of the cross.

"Please do not mention that name here," he urged huskily. "She was not one of my congregation."

"I suppose she was a Catholic," Corynne said doubtfully.

"No, she was not a Catholic," Sallen said in a forced, yet penetrating whisper. "She was evil. If she had a faith at all, she worshipped at the altar of the dark God, Satan. They buried her in sacred soil. I refused to officiate, but they would not heed my protests. She had no place with Christian folk. They desecrated God's place."

He drew himself upright, and stood for a moment looking as he must once have been, tall, strong and proud.

"Jezebel, Harlot, Temptress, Destroyer of men, I knew you for what you were," he declaimed powerfully, then seemed to shrink back into his aged body again."

"Father, what are you doing?"

The old man looked round dazedly, as Roger Sallen came hurrying out of the small doorway. He stopped short at the sight of Corynne.

"Miss West. I do hope my father hasn't been annoying you," he said quickly. "I didn't realize that anyone was here. He can be rather alarming if you don't know him."

"Is he ill?" Corynne asked, watching the old man who had slumped down into one of the pews.

"He had a breakdown, some years ago. He lives in a nursing home now, but I bring him home at week-ends for a visit. He misses the church."

"Is it true? What he said about Marianne Grantham?"

Sallen looked frightened. "What — what — did he say?" he asked tensely.

"He told me he tried to stop her being buried here. Is that true?"

"Yes, I regret to say it is," Sallen answered reluctantly. "He tried to stop Grant from having her buried in the family vault. They had to call in an outside man to officiate. We hushed it all up, he was old and frail, and he should have retired years before."

"That must have been very distressing for you," Corynne said sympathetically.

"It was distressing for everyone involved. I was hoping he'd forgotten it by now."

"I would never have asked him about her if I'd known," Corynne said awkwardly. "I'm so sorry."

"It wasn't your fault. He seems rational enough normally, and he's quite harmless I assure you. We should have seen it coming, I suppose. He was always very strict on morals, and you can imagine what he thought about the laxity of present day behaviour. I think it did something to him, he felt — futile, he kept saying that he'd failed in his vocation."

"I can imagine how today's attitudes upset him," Corynne agreed readily. "He seems such a sweet old man."

"Grant and Marianne were not married in this church, they went to a register office in London. Father considered that they were living in sin, not properly married."

"It sounded to me as though there was more to it than just a general dislike of modern standards." Corynne looked at the old man thoughtfully. "He called Marianne a Jezebel, wanton, temptress, and deceiver of men. Does he think that about all women?"

"No, at least — I don't really know. We try to keep him off the subject," Roger Sallen stammered. He seemed suddenly very uneasy again. "I must get him home. I do apologize most sincerely for any distress he may have caused you."

Corynne watched him hustle the old man out of the church, and followed slowly as they walked ahead of her to the car park. There had been something very strange about Roger Sallen's manner, and she had the beginnings of suspicion about him. She drove back towards Hazelcourt, and by the time she reached the centre her suspicions had crystallized. She turned in at the gates.

Pat Marsh was at the reception desk when she hurried in. "Where's Alan?" she asked urgently.

Pat looked up, startled. "In his office. First door along the corridor, Rynne, what's up? You look as though you've seen a ghost. It's not Mr Grantham, is it?"

"No, he's all right," Corynne told her impatiently. "I must talk to Alan."

"Go in, he's alone."

Corynne did not stop to knock on the door, but burst in. Alan looked up in surprise at her sudden entrance, then got to his feet and walked round the desk towards her.

"Rynne, what's the matter? Why didn't you phone? Has something happened? Is Grant worse?"

"No, no, it's nothing like that," she told him impatiently. "Alan, I've just come from the village. I went to look at the church and Roger Sallen's father was there."

"So?" Alan shrugged. "What are you so excited about?"

"Alan, I think I know who attacked Grant. Do you remember how Roger Sallen suddenly appeared last night? He said he'd had a job to find a parking space, and gone round to the yard."

"What about it?"

"I think he was eavesdropping. I think he heard what you were telling me. What Marianne said about Grant. I think Roger Sallen was her secret lover. His father was raving about Marianne, he called her a Jezebel, harlot, temptress, and deceiver of men. I think he must have known that she and Roger were having an affair, and that made him even more deranged. He refused to take the burial service, didn't he?"

"Yes he did, but . . . " Alan shook his head, clearly bemused by her pronouncement. "I don't know, Rynne," he said jerkily. "Roger's father was disturbed, everyone knew that. He had a complete breakdown. He just couldn't adapt to the stresses of modern life, even in a backwater like Hazelmere. The centre didn't help, so many new people roaming around, and youngsters in shorts and sun-tops everywhere. He must have thought he'd strayed into Sodom or Gomorrah."

"I want to get in touch with that Inspector Phillips who came to see me. Have you got his phone number?"

"Hold your horses, Rynne. You can't go around accusing Roger just because his dad's a bit gaga, Roger's a highly respected man. He's the last person I'd have thought would have been having an affair. Joanne, his wife, isn't very strong, and he would never do anything to hurt her."

"If he was in love with Marianne he might have done anything, even to trying to kill Grant, because he thought Grant had been cruel to her."

"Grant wasn't cruel to her. I tackled him about what she said, and he flatly denied it. I believe him. She must have lied to me for some reason."

"She was jealous of your close

friendship with Grant, possibly. She wanted to spoil things for you both."

"That's what Grant said. He said she threatened to turn everyone against him. She was spiteful and vicious."

"You did a lot of talking."

Alan walked back to his chair and sat down, leaning his arms across the desk. "Grant did most of it. I think he was glad to be able to unburden himself at last. I felt so — guilty. I deserted him just when he needed me most."

"He still needs you," Corynne told him sadly.

"Have you two settled your differences?"

"In a way. I respect his honesty, Alan. He didn't mean to insult me. He . . . " She broke off, wondering if it would be wise to tell Alan more, then thought why not? "He asked me to marry him."

Alan brightened. "Isn't that what you wanted?"

"Yes and no. He offered me a business deal, in effect; a partnership, more than a marriage. He thinks we're well suited."

"You are." There was a hint of regret in Alan's voice.

"Perhaps, but I couldn't accept."

"I'm sorry."

"So am I, but I didn't come here to talk about my problems. I intend to tell Inspector Phillips my suspicions about Roger Sallen, and I thought you ought to know. He's sure to ask you about it. If I'm wrong then I'm sorry, but if you'd heard the way Bartram Sallen spoke about Marianne you'd understand. It was Marianne, not women in general he was condemning."

"How can you be so sure?"

"I doubt if anyone had dared raise the subject with him, until I rushed in like the proverbial fool, and asked him about her point blank. I probably wouldn't have done it if I'd known his history, so I'm very glad that no one ever told me."

"You must do what you think right,

Rynne, but I think you're mistaken. Roger Sallen of all people! It's just not possible."

"I agree that it seems unlikely, Alan, that's why no one ever suspected him, but he was scared when he came out and found his father talking to me. There's no proof, I know, but I have a feeling . . . "

"Feminine intuition," Alan laughed hollowly.

"Laugh if you like, but I must talk to the Inspector. Have you got his telephone number?"

"I've got it." Alan gave in, and flicked through his phone index, dialled and asked for the Inspector, then handed the receiver to her.

Phillips listened in silence to what she had to say, then thanked her for her information. He said he would be calling later to talk to her.

She gave the phone back to Alan, and stood up.

"Thank you, Alan. I'm sorry if you think I'm stirring up trouble, but I couldn't just ignore my suspicions."

"It is possible that you could have stumbled onto something that those of us more familiar with events missed," he admitted grudgingly.

"Thanks, Alan."

"Would you like a coffee?" he offered.

"No thanks, I'd better be getting back. Martha will never forgive me if I'm late for dinner," she said lightly, and hurried out.

She felt a little guilty that she might have caused some unpleasantness for Roger Sallen, but she was determined to do everything that she could to find out the truth about Marianne's past, for Grant's sake.

11

WHEN she got back to Hazel-court House, Corynne went straight upstairs to freshen up for dinner. She had just reached her own room when the door of Grant's opened, and he stood looking at her defiantly.

"Where do you think you're going?" she asked coldly, then realized that it might be a tactless question.

He drew his robe round himself, and tightened the sash almost protectively, and she had to laugh at the schoolboyish guilt in his expression.

"What's funny?" he growled.

"You were about to sneak downstairs," she accused.

"What if I was? I'm all right . . . "

"You won't be if you don't do as Bill Hallam told you, and rest. If you want something I'll get it for you, just ring the bell. I shall be in the kitchen with Martha."

"I didn't want to bother her. She's too old to be running up and down stairs . . . "

"That's why *I* shall come. Now, back to bed." She clapped her hands smartly, as though she was scolding a naughty puppy.

He was so startled that he turned and shuffled back into his room, sulkily climbing into the bed, and leaning back with his arms folded. Trying not to laugh she tucked him in, and straightened the covers.

"What did you want?"

"Coffee," he said dully. "I'm longing for a cup of strong black coffee. I suppose that's forbidden too?"

"No, if it's coffee you want, you shall have it."

"Corynne, I'm sorry if I upset you again. I didn't intend to. I meant what I said. Don't be too hasty about turning me down," he said jerkily. "Think about it please."

"It wouldn't do any good if I did," she told him. "You know my answer, Grant. I can't marry you unless you're sure that you love me, no matter how I feel about you. If you can't make that commitment then you obviously don't. Please don't make things any more difficult than they are."

"Get the coffee, damn you," he grated, and let his head rest back on the pillow wearily.

She brought him the coffee, and several other things that he rang to ask for, and carried his dinner up on a tray, maintaining a brisk professional manner, and refusing to let him shake her new-found composure.

The rest of the day passed swiftly. Alan called during the evening, and Inspector Phillips made a brief visit to ask her a few details. He seemed quite impressed by what she told him, and left, promising to let them know if there were any developments.

On Monday she began her duties as Mrs Grantham's secretary, and was kept surprisingly busy. Her work was occasionally interrupted by a summons from Grant, during the morning, but after lunch Bill Hallam called, and declared him fit to come downstairs.

She dined with him that evening, and the conversation was strained, both of them carefully avoiding the subject that was uppermost in their minds. His mother did not join them, pleading a headache, but Corynne suspected that she had deliberately left them alone together, hoping that they could sort something out.

On Tuesday morning Bill Hallam visited his patient, and agreed that Grant could return to London and his office that afternoon.

They had lunch together, and she waited in vain for him to say that he was sorry to be leaving.

"I'll be in touch," he said casually at the door. "Let me know your decision about staying or leaving when the month's trial is up, that is assuming that mother wants you to stay, of course. Her decision is final."

She watched him drive off in the red sports car with mixed feelings, and tried to settle down to the routine of life at Hazelcourt.

The days were filled with business, shopping, fetching books from Hazelbury library, and sometimes driving Mrs Grantham around, when she felt well enough.

In the evenings and at week-ends she often went out with Julie, if Bill was working, and they quickly became close friends. Alan was a frequent visitor to the house, and it was Alan who brought the news, some four weeks after the attack on Grant.

"Rynne, prepare yourself for a shock," he said, walking into her office on the Friday morning.

She looked up from the account books that she had been working on. "What's happened?" she asked, alarmed by his manner.

"I've just come from the Sallen's, Joanne called me. Roger was found drowned this morning."

"Oh no, poor Joanne, how dreadful," she said huskily. "How did it happen?"

"He killed himself. He's admitted that he was the man who attacked Grant. He left a letter begging Joanne to forgive him. Phillips had questioned him, and it frightened him. He said that he couldn't live with his conscience any longer. He realized what a terrible thing he'd done, and was taking the honourable way out to save Joanne the horror of a trial."

"Alan, that's awful," Corynne whispered. "Even if he was guilty, he needn't have . . . "

"He did what he thought best, Rynne. He's confessed to everything. The smear campaign in the papers, the attacks on Grant, even to something that you never suspected him of."

"Something else?"

"Yes. He killed Marianne, or at least he was responsible for her death. That night, when Marianne told Grant she was going for a swim, she'd arranged to meet Roger in that hut on the beach. After they'd made love she told him that he wasn't man enough to satisfy her, and she didn't want to see him again. She said he wasn't worth the risk she was taking, if Grant found out about them."

"What a cruel thing to say."

"Yes, it was," Alan agreed grimly. "Her cruelty killed her. She threatened to tell everyone that he'd been pestering her. She said that she had to be sure that Grant didn't blame her. She was afraid of what he might do if he found out."

"Alan, that's awful. Sallen must have been shattered."

"He was. He knew he was finished if the story got out, and she was standing there laughing at him. In his own words — 'something seemed to crack inside his head'. He grabbed her, but she broke away from him, and ran out onto the rocks. He chased her, and she lost her footing and fell into the water. She must have hit her head as she fell. By the time he got her out she was dead and he panicked and ran away."

"And he's lived with that secret for two years. Alan, I can almost feel sorry for him, if it hadn't been for what he did to Grant. Why was he so bitter?"

"He was infuriated with her. Somehow he blamed Grant for her death. She'd told him that Grant bullied her, and refused to divorce her."

"What nonsense," Corynne declared. "More likely she didn't want to leave him; she knew when she was well off."

"Grant told me that he'd asked her to divorce him, and she'd refused. She threatened to claim custody of the children, and prove that he wasn't fit to get near them, if he tried to divorce her."

"She did all she could to hurt Grant, didn't she? Even after she was dead her lies went on working. He gave her a good home, she couldn't have lacked for anything. How could she have been so vindictive?"

"We shall never know that, Rynne. But at last he really does have a chance to come to terms with the past now that the truth is out. He wasn't the only man she deceived and tormented, and he certainly wasn't to blame for her death. He's got to accept that it was Marianne at fault, not him."

"Oh Alan, I hope so," Corynne breathed. "I'm sorry that it had to end so tragically, but I'm happy for Grant. He's suffered so much. Does he know yet?"

"Yes, I phoned him before I came over. He's driving down tomorrow afternoon. Expect him for dinner."

Corynne felt a moment of elation, then the doubts returned. She wondered how she could face him again. The anguish of love had diminished a little with him away, but what would it be like to meet him face to face again, remembering all that had happened between them?

"I thought you'd be pleased," Alan said doubtfully, when she did not respond.

"I am, but I'm scared too, about meeting him again. And what will the papers make of Sallen's death? Will there be a lot more muck-raking?"

"If there is, at least Grant won't be the target. I don't know how much information Phillips will let the papers have, but he's a good man, and he'll see that justice is done, and seen to be done, I'm sure."

"I do hope so. I couldn't bear it if Grant had to go through all that again."

"For all his good works, Roger Sallen has never been very well-liked in the village. Just remember that Grant will be the injured party this time. Roger was having an affair with his wife, and accidentally killed her. He's admitted it. Roger knew what he was doing when he drowned himself. He took the easy way out. He'd probably have faced a manslaughter charge at the least. In the end he did his best to save Joanne from more distress."

"Yes, a trial would have been worse for everyone," Corynne agreed.

"I must be getting back, but I simply had to tell you the news in person, before it got garbled through the local grapevine."

"Thank you, Alan. I appreciate that."

"Will you tell Mrs Grantham for me, and tell her I'll call in and see her some time this afternoon. I have to get back to the centre now."

"Yes, of course. Thanks again, Alan."

Corynne saw him out and went in to tell Grant's mother the news. Mrs Grantham was delighted to know that she would no longer have to fear for Grant's safety, but her joy was tinged with regret for Joanne Sallen, who she knew well.

Over lunch Corynne had to tell the story all over again for Martha.

"I never did like that Roger Sallen," Martha said, unusually harshly for her.

"Never could see what Joanne saw in him. Smarmy little toad I called him. Oh well, shouldn't speak ill of the dead. Leastways he had the decency to save us all a lot more trouble. May he rest in peace, though he don't deserve to."

Corynne was forced to agree with her.

The rest of the day passed with wearisome slowness. Saturday was even more difficult. She was free to please herself at week-ends, unless there was anything essential to attend to, and time hung heavily.

She kept thinking about how the news would affect Grant. Would it finally convince him that he had nothing to blame himself for? He was not the only man who Marianne had cruelly deceived.

She dressed for dinner that evening with care, choosing the same green dress that she had worn on her first evening at Hazelcourt. Somehow it seemed appropriate.

She went downstairs to the sitting-room early, and settled herself to await his arrival, determined to appear calm and unaffected. The crunch of tyres on the gravel made her heart pound uncomfortably, and by the time she heard his footsteps crossing the hall she was atingle with anticipation.

"I'd hoped to find you here," he said easily, as he opened the door and strode in.

She looked up from the magazine that she was pretending to read.

"Hallo, Grant," she greeted him. "How is business?"

He seemed rather taken aback by her composure. "Busy," he said rather abruptly. "How is Hazelcourt?"

"Fine. Your mother is keeping well, and I've even persuaded her to come for a drive with me a few times. I think you'll find everything in order. By the way, I don't know if you realized it, but my month's trial ended yesterday, and she asked me to take the position permanently."

"Are you going to?"

"Yes. I like working for your mother, and I like Hazelcourt, and the village. It's just the kind of peaceful place I'd hoped for."

"Good."

They were sparring with each other, both determined to keep the conversation safe, Corynne realized. But there were things that had to be said.

"Have you seen the local papers?"

"No. I didn't stop to pick one up."

"Here." She picked up the paper that lay on the table, and held it out to him. He took it, and sat in the armchair opposite her.

SHOCK CONFESSION OF LOCAL CHURCHMAN. He read the headline aloud.

Church organist and scoutmaster Roger Sallen was found drowned early on Friday morning on the small beach close to the village of Hazelmere. He left his wife Joanne a letter, confessing to having

240

caused the death of Mrs Marianne Grantham, wife of local businessman Grant Grantham, two years ago. He also admitted carrying out a campaign of hate against Mr Grantham, and was apparently responsible for a number of false reports about Mr Grantham's activities, and also a number of attacks on Mr Grantham himself, culminating in a recent murder attempt.

The proprietor of this paper wishes to make a public apology to Mr Grantham. Every item printed in this newspaper is checked and verified as far as possible, but items received from reliable sources are accepted in good faith. The proprietor deeply regrets any distress caused to Mr Grantham by such items.

"Isn't it wonderful?" Corynne asked eagerly. "They've actually apologized."

"I can hardly believe it." Grant dropped the paper onto the table, looking dazed. "Someone pulled a lot of strings to get that article published, and I suspect I know who."

Corynne smiled. "Alan?"

"Yes, Alan."

"It's over, Grant. All the suspicion and gossip is over."

"I'm almost afraid to believe it."

He stood up and walked to the window, staring out blankly. "I've been in a daze ever since Alan told me yesterday. I understand that it was thanks to you that Phillips got on to Sallen." He half-turned, and looked at her thoughtfully. "I'm grateful."

"I'm just so glad that I was able to help, but I do wish that it hadn't ended so tragically. Poor Joanne. She must be dreadfully upset."

"I thought I loved Marianne once," he said grimly. "I thought she loved me. How could I have been so wrong?"

"Alan told you why Roger Sallen killed her, I suppose?"

He moved towards her slowly. "Yes, he told me. Marianne could be so convincing, but she lied about everything.

She could destroy a man with words. Our marriage was a mockery from the start. If I tried to make love to her she accused me of wanting nothing else. She said I was too demanding. In the end — I believed her."

"That was why you wanted to be so sure that I'd been willing, that first time you — kissed me."

"Yes," he said huskily.

Corynne said shakily, "I can understand it all now. Why you've behaved the way you have. Marianne used sex as a weapon against men."

Grant nodded grimly. "I put up with her for the sake of the children, I wanted to give them a good home, and I didn't think she would care for them properly if I divorced her. I couldn't risk her getting custody. I loved them, but they were strangers. They spoke a foreign language. She taught them to hate me . . . "

"It's over, done with," Corynne said, alarmed by his intensity. She wanted to run to him, and hold him try to comfort him. It wasn't over for him, not quite, even now.

He took a step closer, and she stood up to meet him.

"She took everything I could give her, and gave nothing in return," he said bitterly. "Why? Why?"

"She wasn't capable of love," Corynne told him gently. "She only wanted to hurt people. Bertram Sallen said she was evil. He said she had a heathen soul, that was why he wouldn't officiate at the funeral."

"He was so right."

"Grant, it wasn't only you. She hated all men. Perhaps she had a reason. She certainly had a strange power. Even Alan believed her for a time. There aren't many women like her, thank God."

He stared at her as though he was awakening from a nightmare. Slowly the grey shadows of despair lifted from his eyes, and they shone clear and blue.

"Corynne," he said softly. "I had to

244

be sure. I've had time to think, these past few weeks, and I am sure now. I . . . "

"Not yet," she whispered, laying her fingers on his mouth to silence him. She thought that she knew what he had been about to say, but she didn't want to hear it, not yet. "You'd better go and let your mother know you're here, then dinner will be ready."

"Yes, of course," he smiled, and bent his head to kiss her gently on the mouth. It was such a different sensation from the hard demanding kisses she remembered, and she put her hands up to cradle his face, and returned the kiss with the same tender pressure. His arms went round her, and for a moment the old passion returned, then he let go, and moved away from her.

"Not yet," he repeated her words softly, and walked out of the room.

She was content to wait, sharing the meal with him, and afterwards, when his mother joined them, they talked of Hazelmere, the conference centre, and the future, as yet undefined, and rich with plans as yet unformed. Mrs Grantham seemed very aware that something was happening, but wisely asked no questions, and it was barely ten o'clock when she asked Corynne to help her to bed.

When she went back to the sitting-room Grant was standing by the fireplace. He had switched on the electric fire, and the room was gently lit by the flicker of artificial flames. He smiled as she closed the door and walked towards him, stopping at arm's length.

"Is it time?" he asked throatily.

"Yes, it's time."

He reached her in one swift stride, and his arms crushed her against his chest. His lips found hers, and his kiss brought fire to her body, and a heady weakness to her limbs. She was no longer afraid of his strength, and surrendered willingly to his passion, sharing it, and returning it, with the depths of a love that had been waiting for this moment.

When he lifted his head and looked down at her, the shadows had gone for ever.

"Corynne, I'm sure now that I love you," he said confidently, with such a vibrancy in his voice. "Will you marry me?"

"Oh my darling, I love you so very, very much," she whispered. "Yes, I'll marry you."

THE END

WITH SOMEBODY ELSE
Theresa Charles

Rosamond sets off for Cornwall with Hugo to meet his family, blissfully unaware of the shocks in store for her.

A SUMMER FOR STRANGERS
Claire Hamilton

Because she had lost her job, her flat and she had no money, Tabitha agreed to pose as Adam's future wife although she believed the scheme to be deceitful and cruel.

VILLA OF SINGING WATER
Angela Petron

The disquieting incidents that occurred at the Vatican and the Colosseum did not trouble Jan at first, but then they became increasingly unpleasant and alarming.

DOCTOR NAPIER'S NURSE
Pauline Ash

When cousins Midge and Derry are entered as probationer nurses on the same day but at different hospitals they agree to exchange identities.

A GIRL LIKE JULIE
Louise Ellis

Caroline absolutely adored Hugh Barrington, but then Julie Crane came into their lives. Julie was the kind of girl who attracts men without even trying.

COUNTRY DOCTOR
Paula Lindsay

When Evan Richmond bought a practice in a remote country village he did not realise that a casual encounter would lead to the loss of his heart.